beginnings

Welcome to Prima New Beginnings

Prima New Beginnings is all about women
facing up to the glorious unpredictability
of life – warm and compelling stories that
are relevant for every woman who has
ever sought to open a new chapter or
wondered "What's next?".

**Because every life has more
than one chapter.**

In *Prima Magazine* there is something for
everyone – advice on how to look and feel
your best, time- and money-saving solutions,
quick-and-easy food, beautiful homes and
gardens and, above all, everything you
need to make your life simple.

MILLS & BOON®

Nancy Robards Thompson has reinvented herself numerous times. In the process, she's worked at a myriad of jobs, including newspaper reporting; television show stand-in; production and casting extras for movies; and several mind-numbing jobs in the fashion industry and public relations. She earned a degree in journalism, only to realise that reporting "just the facts" bored her silly. Much more content to report to her muse, Nancy has found nirvana doing what she loves most – writing romance fiction full-time. Since hanging up her press pass, this two-time nominee for the Romance Writers of America's Golden Heart struck gold in July 2002 when she won the award. She lives in Orlando, Florida, with her husband, Michael, their daughter, and three cats, but that doesn't stop her from dreaming of a life as a bohemian writer in Paris.

OUT WITH THE OLD, IN WITH THE NEW

Nancy Robards Thompson

MILLS & BOON®

First published in Great Britain 2007
by Harlequin Mills & Boon Limited, Eton House,
18-24 Paradise Road,
Richmond, Surrey TW9 1SR

© Nancy Robards Thompson 2005

ISBN: 978 0 263 85868 6

39-0507

Printed and bound in Spain
by Litografia Rosés S.A., Barcelona

From the Author

Dear Reader,

I read recently that forty is the new thirty. What does that mean? That forty was considered over the hill and is no longer as old as once perceived? Or is it reflective of a new attitude? That chronological age is irrelevant and a woman can reinvent herself at any age?

The latter is the premise of my story *Out with the Old, In with the New*. When forty-year-old Kate Hennessey discovers her marriage of twenty years is over, she's faced with the horrifying realisation that she gave half her life to a man who doesn't want her any more. At first, she worries the breakup means the best years of her life – and all she's accomplished in that time – are null and void. Learning to stand on her own two feet, she embraces her new path and the opportunity to grow into her full potential.

I hope you enjoy Kate's journey of self-discovery. Here's wishing you a lifetime of love and happiness…and the strength to look deep inside yourself and discover where those qualities live.

Warmly,

Nancy Robards Thompson

This book is dedicated to the transforming
power of friendship and to my good friends
Katherine Garbera, Mary Louise Wells,
Teresa Brown, Elizabeth Grainger,
Catherine Kean, Debbie Pfeiffer, Robin Trimble,
Joanne Maio, Carol Reiss, Evelyn Sechler and
Christina Mancia.
Ladies, your friendship makes my life very rich.

Acknowledgements

First and foremost, I'd like to thank two wonderful
women – Michelle Grajkowski, my agent, and
Gail Chasan, my editor. Michelle, thanks for
having the foresight to get this manuscript into
Gail's hands. Gail, thanks for everything.
I look forward to many years of collaboration
with both of you.

Heartfelt appreciation (and a long overdue dinner)
to Robert Trimble for your sage advice on divorce
law (for the book, thank God, not for real life!).

Finally, love and thanks to Michael and Jennifer.
I couldn't do this without your love and support.

CHAPTER 1

Confession time. I'm not going on the annual girls' weekend with Alex and Rainey. But how do you tell your best friends you're breaking a ten-year tradition because you don't trust your husband enough to leave him alone for two nights?

It's embarrassing. Humiliating.

Rainey would hate Corbin if she thought he was having an affair. And Alex—she'd kill him. Then they'd both rally around me, like a prizefighter's coaches who were training for the kill.

I'm not ready to deal with it. Saying it out loud makes it so…real.

I can hear Alex now. "Kate, if he's cheating, your staying in town isn't going to stop him. So you can't miss our weekend." And that would inevitably prompt her to add, "If you even *think* he's cheating, why don't you hire a private detective and find out for sure?"

Don't think I haven't considered hiring someone. But for God's sake, it hasn't even been a full twenty-four hours since the bomb dropped. I need time to think, to sort out my options and figure out how to deal with the aftermath, should I discover the man I sleep with every night is being unfaithful.

This ugly jealousy is so new. All I can think of is this time yesterday I trusted my husband. I loved him and was so sure he loved me.

Right now, I don't even know my next move. Let me figure that out first. Then I'll sic Alex on him.

So instead of leveling with them, I resort to diversionary tactics. "Palm Beach is too stuffy." I sink into the couch cushions and slant a glance at Rainey. I catch her almost imperceptible eye roll.

"Come *on*, Kate." Alex scowls at me. "You've managed to pooh-pooh every suggestion we've made tonight. South Beach is too wild. Palm Springs is too boring. Napa's too far." She says this in a singsong voice that makes me want to jump out of my skin. "New York's too... What was wrong with New York?"

I shouldn't have come tonight, but after what happened today, I've been running on autopilot, trying to regain my equilibrium. Quite unsuccessfully, I might add. So I can't blame them for being annoyed. I'd be irritated with me, too. Especially since this girls' getaway is the last one we'll take as *thirty-somethings*.

Yep, the big four-oh looms right down the pike. For each of us, one right after the other. Boom, boom, boom. I'm the first of the three to cross that dubious threshold in May. Alex turns right after me in August—

Turns.

Turns? That's horrible. It sounds like one day we're light and lively and the next day we're soured milk. I'd never thought of it that way and wish I hadn't, because it gives me yet another reason to dread *turning* forty. Anyhow, Rainey is the baby of the bunch, the last of us to outlive her shelf life. She *turns* in November.

We started the annual girls' getaway the year of our thirtieth birthdays. So in a sense this year is a double celebration—ten years of annual getaways and our foray into the fabulous forties. I guess that makes me a double party pooper.

"Must we decide this tonight? It's late." I stand up and prepare to leave, ignoring the pair of disapproving looks. Rainey levels me with a stare that screams *stop being so difficult*.

"Palm Beach is perfect. It has spas and shopping.

What more could we ask for? All in favor of Palm Beach?"

As I pull my car keys from my bag, the two of them raise their hands, voting yes, looking at me with equal parts exasperation and impatience.

I hitch my Coach bag onto my shoulder. "Okay, fine. Palm Beach. Whatever."

At this point, I'll agree to anything, even though I have no intention of actually going. I just want to leave before the walls close in on me. Later, I'll think of a plausible excuse to bow out of the trip. Maybe I'll even tell the truth.

Ha. The truth. What a novel idea.

I don't have to tell them about my suspicions, mind you. The other truth is that my six-year-old, Caitlin, hates it when I go away, which is not very often. So I can't go because Corbin's not a good babysitter. He's a good dad, and Caitlin loves him as if he were a prince. But when it comes to bedtime, she wants me.

God, that's lame. They'll never buy it.

Well, we're all adults. Alex and Rainey will understand. Eventually.

Alex makes a satisfied noise. "This is going to be a blast." She does a little merengue step. "We're going to get every imaginable spa treatment known to womankind, then we're going to par-tay and we're going to shop— Oh, Kate, that reminds me, I still have your pearls. Let me run upstairs and get them before you go."

She's out of the room before I can tell her not to worry about it. Rainey and I stand face-to-face for an awkward moment. I can tell she's going to ask what's bugging me. So I drop my purse onto the chair, pick up my champagne flute and carry it to the kitchen.

She follows me.

The room is too small for both of us and the pregnant questions wedged between.

I keep my back to her and wash my glass.

"Are you all right?" she finally asks. "You haven't been yourself all night."

"I'm fine. Tired."

My composure wavers. In my mind's eye I see hysteria reaching up to trip me, yanking my poise out from under me like an old rug. I have that sense of slow-motion disorientation, like when you see yourself suspended in midair a split second before a hard fall.

But I'm still standing.

If I stand perfectly still, not moving or speaking or breathing, I will not go down.

I will *not* come undone.

For a full minute I let the water run over my hands and stare at the vivid cobalt and yellow in the Spanish tile backsplash behind Alex's kitchen sink.

My eyes haven't teared. No surprise. For the past twelve hours, I've felt as if I were locked inside a wooden cask of a body, incapable of emotion. Numbed by the hard exterior that's settled around me.

Movement reflected in the kitchen window catches my eye. I see Rainey's reflection. She's just standing there. Not pushing or needling or prodding. Somehow, without even looking directly at her, I sense she's reaching out through the murky stillness. I know in that instant I could fall backward, and she wouldn't let me hit the ground. But I can't right now. I just can't.

I turn to her and say, "I'm fine, Rainey. Really."

Alex enters with my pearls. They were an anniversary gift from Corbin. She drops them into my hand, and I get the absurd vision that they're an abacus tallying Corbin's transgressions.

One precious pearl for each sin against our marriage. I'm sober enough to realize I'm just tipsy enough to let my imagination run rampant, but I'm okay to drive. I wouldn't get behind the wheel otherwise.

Fingering the pearls, I grab my purse, say good-night

and escape into the chilly cloak of moonless night, wishing it would swallow me whole so I wouldn't have to go home and face my husband.

During my twenty-minute drive to Winter Park I realize I need to come up with a game plan. I've had since ten o'clock this morning when the mail arrived to think about it. Yet I still can't force myself to go there. What in the world am I going to say to Corbin when I get home?

"Sweetheart, I received the strangest letter in the mail today. It said, 'Ask your husband what he's been doing all those nights he claimed to be at the hospital.'" Then I'll laugh to prove I'm confident the note's a prank.

Then he'll laugh, and it will become our own private joke. He'll pull me into bed and make love to me to show me how absurd the letter was.

We haven't made love in months. Why would tonight be any different? Especially when I'm pretty sure he's not going to be overly thrilled about getting his own dinner. When it came time to go out, I fed Caitlin and let her go play at the neighbor's house. I was in such a fog I didn't even think about fixing his dinner. I hope I locked the door.

I can't think straight for all the bells and whistles

sounding in my head warning that something's rotten in the Hennessey household. If I ignore my gut feeling I'll be just like all the other pathetic women who know damn well their husbands are screwing around, but pretend they don't have a clue so they can keep the big house and the fancy cars and the summertime trips to Tuscany. How can they live knowing their whole life is a sham?

I look at the dashboard clock glowing azure. I now have approximately ten minutes to concoct a plan. Most likely he'll be asleep. Do I wake him up and confront him? Throw the letter in his face and scream, "What the fuck have you been doing?"

I shudder. I hate that word. I hate feeling compelled to ask him to account for his time. But most of all, I want him to know I hate playing the fool.

I could wake him and ask, "So, Corbin, what have you been doing lately?"

Ha. I can see it now. He'll blink because he's sleepy, then he'll look at me as if I'm an idiot and repeat the question back to me. "What have I been doing lately, Kate?"

He'll tick off a list of noble and important deeds. You know, a typical surgeon's fourteen-hour day. It won't be what he says that hurts, but how he says it. Especially when he adds his favorite line: "That was my day, Kate. What did *you* do today?"

And I'll say, "Well, Corbin, today I pondered why someone would send me a letter encouraging me to ask you what you do with yourself. But if it were any other day, I'd probably have to stop and think, God, what *did* I do today? It certainly slipped by fast. When itemized, my list would be just as long as yours, I'm sure. But since I'm just a mom and a typical day for me revolves around the PTA and organizing school bake sales and timing my life to have dinner ready in between running our daughter to two-hour dance classes and peewee cheerleading lessons, I didn't have time to discover the cure for AIDS and the common cold, much less screw around on you. Certainly not as complex as a doctor's day, but my life is full."

I steer the car off the interstate and as I coast to a stop at the light at Fairbanks and Highway 17-92, I realize I've been talking to myself—out loud. There's a couple in a black Corvette in the lane next to me, but they're making out, oblivious to my self-banter and my watching them go at it.

If Corbin does have a girlfriend, where do they rendezvous? A cheap motel? Her place? In the car? I surprise myself at how I can ponder the possibilities so calmly. I suppose the logistics would depend on the bimbo.

God, who is she?

Do I know her?

Someone in his office? The hospital? The country club? Someone I've invited into my home? That would be the worst. The champagne bubbles up sourly in the back of my throat. I take a few deep breaths and remind myself this whole thing could be a hoax.

"A hoax."

I say the words aloud hoping they will ring true. But my gut instinct doesn't buy it.

Somehow I know.

I just know.

The light turns green, and I stomp on the gas pedal. The wheels scream as I lurch into the intersection. There's something satisfying about the obnoxious sound. Like steam screaming through the release valve on a pressure cooker. I hope the noise startled the kissing couple in the Corvette enough to make them knock noses.

A few minutes later, I steer my Lexus SUV into the driveway and hit the garage door opener. I wait for the door to lift and notice the glow of the living-room lights seeping through the slats of the plantation shutters, as though a happy family lives here. Maybe Corbin's still awake. A wave of panic seizes me, and I can't breathe for a few seconds.

But I force air into my lungs. I still have no idea what I'm going to say to him, but I decide right then and there I'm not going to make it easy for him. Girls' get-away be damned. Going out of town with Alex and Rainey would be like handing him a free pass to be with her.

Whoever she is.

I pull into the garage, kill the engine and sit there until the door wheezes and squeaks shut behind me. Once closed, the garage is perfectly silent, except for the occasional tick and sigh of the car's hot engine.

If I really want to know who she is I can find out.

The thought makes my heart beat so fast it hurts. I take a deep breath to calm myself, run my hand over the tan glove leather of the passenger seat. I need to touch something tangible, something tactile, to ground me in reality.

I love this car. It was Corbin's present to me three months ago for our twentieth anniversary. He picked it out himself. Had it delivered with a big red bow on the hood. Like something you'd see in a television commercial.

If material gifts were a standard of measure for his love, there would be no doubt. Always generous. A good provider. And a good father.

Because of that, doesn't he deserve the benefit of the doubt? Or at least a chance to explain?

The beginning of a headache buzzes in my temples. I close my eyes and press my fingers against the lids, but it doesn't help. When I open my eyes again, the dim overhead light casts an eerie yellow glow. Everything looks fuzzy and out of proportion, especially the shadows.

If I shine a bright light directly into the darkness, will I prove this dread is merely a figment of my imagination?

As my eyes focus, I see Caitlin's in-line skates hanging on the Peg-Board next to the kitchen door. Corbin's golf clubs sit below. My treadmill, slightly dusty, is next to it. Our three bikes are suspended by chains from the ceiling.

Am I willing to give it all up so easily because of an anonymous letter containing one vague sentence?

A chill winds its way through my body. Despite the cool January-in-Florida weather, the night air feels clammy and clings to me like a bad omen.

Okay, I'll ask him.

I'll ask him because I *need* Corbin to explain this away. Not so I can turn the other cheek while he fools around. I want him to convince me it's not true for the sake of our family.

For the twenty years I've given him.

God, that's half my life.

I let myself out of the car. As I put my key in the kitchen door, I hear Jack, our yellow Lab, barking before I let myself inside. He jumps up to greet me as I step into the kitchen.

"Shh, Jack. Be quiet. You're going to wake the whole house." I stroke his silky head half hoping, half fearing Corbin will call out to me that he's in the living room. But he doesn't.

The dirty dinner dishes are still on the table along with the remnants of Chinese takeout. I flip off the kitchen light.

My heels click on the hardwood floor as I walk into the living room. Is every light in the house on?

"Corbin?"

The house is so still my words seem to echo back at me. I turn off the downstairs lights and make my way upstairs, which is completely dark by contrast. I push open Caitlin's bedroom door. Her night-light glows in the corner.

She's sleeping on her stomach like an angel child in her pink canopy bed. Long, curly blond hair flows around her. She looks like a princess floating on a spun-gold cloud.

As far as her daddy's concerned, she is a princess. Although he wasn't exactly thrilled when I found out I was pregnant. Caitlin was a surprise. Our son, Daniel, was thirteen when she was born, and Corbin was ready to "have his life back," as he put it. We were going to travel, and he wanted more time for golf.

Secretly, I was thrilled to be pregnant again. I'd miscarried three times after Daniel was born. Then I quit conceiving.

I just knew she'd be a girl. Not that I don't love my son. I do. I just always wanted a baby girl. And now that Daniel's away at college, it's great having someone who still needs me. See, she was meant to be.

That's what I kept telling Corbin and, of course, the minute she was born she had him wrapped around her little finger. So it's been a moot point ever since. I mean what's not to love?

She just turned six. It's a wonderful age. Every age is

wonderful, but this one is particularly nice. She's so sweet, and there's nothing I'd rather do than be her mother.

Is that so bad? Does it make me unambitious to find fulfillment in motherhood?

I suppose I should add *wife* to that job description. But it goes without saying.

Doesn't it?

I stroke a wisp of hair off Caitlin's forehead and realize with startling clarity as if I'm staring back through a tunnel of years that mine and Corbin's relationship went a little off track when I got pregnant. I guess we haven't had a chance to reconnect as we should have. But you know how it is having a new baby. Since then, life set sail on its own course. Corbin's practice has just been named the staff physicians for Orlando Magic— the NBA team—and he's busier than ever at the hospital. Sometimes I've felt as if all I can do is hold on or risk falling overboard.

But now everything's run aground because of that damned letter.

My heart aches. I kiss Caitlin's cheek and linger to inhale her sweet scent, but she stirs, and I pull back so I don't wake her.

I walk down the dark hall, into our darker bedroom. I click on the overhead light. Corbin's asleep on his side. His back is to me. When I sit on the side of the bed, my thigh grazes his body.

I touch his bare shoulder. He lets out a little snore. "Corbin, wake up. We need to talk."

CHAPTER 2

I remember a time when a *pickup line* was defined as a lustful attempt to make somebody's acquaintance. For the past nineteen years, the only *pickup line* I've been party to is the slow-moving, after-school queue that snakes around the Liberty School parking lot.

I don't miss being hit on. What bothers me as I sit waiting for my daughter to get out of school is the fact that I never noticed the incongruous dual usage of the term.

Pickup line.

It's so ridiculous. How could I have missed it?

It makes me wonder what else I've overlooked all these years.

I trust so freely. I mean, why shouldn't I? If a person—namely my husband—has never given me reason to doubt him, why shouldn't I trust him implicitly? It can't be any other way. A relationship without trust is a derailed train.

No. Worse.

It's a yawning sinkhole that opens its greedy jaws and devours everything that once seemed stable. Without trust, you might as well end it before the relationship gets ugly.

Because it will. Without trust, sooner or later you'll end up eating each other alive.

That's why when Corbin pronounced the letter someone's idea of a sick joke, I chose to believe him.

I had to.

If you could have seen him, his eyes hooded and heavy with sleep. He propped himself up on his elbow and blinked at the paper I thrust in his face. "What's this?"

The overhead light cast shadows on his face, hollowing his cheeks, making his cheekbones appear even sharper. So handsome. What woman wouldn't want him?

"I don't know, Corbin. I was hoping you could explain it to me."

The memory seems ancient, as though it happened years ago, but it still shakes me to the core. I move up three car lengths, edging closer, but not too close, to the Volvo station wagon in front of me, then pull the lapels of my navy-blue peacoat closed at my neck and wait in stone-cold silence for the *pickup line* to inch its way around to Caitlin. The radio's off because every time I turned it on they were playing songs like "Fifty Ways to Leave Your Lover," and "How am I Supposed to Live Without You." When was the last time I heard those ditties?

I glance in the rearview mirror. The line of cars stretches back to infinity.

I'm gridlocked.

Even if I wanted to get out of this line, I couldn't. If I were in a better mood I might make a wry comparison about how gridlock reminds me of marriage.

I can't leave him. I mean, my God, we've been married for twenty years.

Half my life.

Whoa. I will not waste my energy by contemplating divorce. Corbin's not having an affair. Period.

Last night he caved in over the note, as if someone punched him in the stomach. He held his head in his hands and said, *"What the hell...? This is bullshit. Kate? You don't think—?"*

"I don't know what to think, Corbin."

I stood there with my hands on my hips acting like

such a bitch—for about thirty seconds. Then all I wanted to do was beg him, *Tell me it isn't true, Corbin. Make me believe this isn't true*.

But I couldn't say it because I knew I should either believe in him…or leave him. Asking him to tell me it isn't true is like admitting I don't trust him.

Feeling the sinkhole rumble underneath me, I sit in the midst of *pickup line* gridlock, stuck in my own personal gridlock because I can't write off the letter as a hoax. I won't let myself slide down into the what-ifs of extramarital affair investigation.

You know—A plus B plus C equals Corbin's opportunity to cheat. Oh, and remember that time that he should have been home at six, but didn't get in until eleven-thirty—

La! La! La! La! La! La! La! I can't hear me! Don't want to hear me because my husband is *not* having an affair.

That's better. I lean my head against the cool window. Try on the words for size: I believe him.

I want to believe in the way he reached out last night, took my arm and pulled me down next to him on the bed.

"Kate, look at me."

He tried to lace his fingers through mine, but I jerked away and traced the burnished gold-on-gold woven into the raw silk of our duvet cover. Until he pounded the bed. "Goddamn it, Kate. Come on. This is fucking bullshit."

I pounded the bed, too. "Don't yell at me, Corbin! This is not my fault."

Tell me it isn't true. Make me believe this isn't true.

He held up a hand. Squeezed his eyes shut. Drew in a deep breath through flaring nostrils. "I'm sorry, let's just start over. From the beginning. Where's the envelope?"

The plain white rectangle lay kitty-corner, half on the hardwood floor, half on the Persian rug next to the bed. The white stood out like a surrender flag against a blood-orange sunset.

Corbin picked up the envelope. Flipped it from one side to the other. Snorted. "Nothing."

A quick flick of his wrist, sent the envelope skimming across the polished wood until it dead-ended into the baseboard.

Then we sat side-by-side in silence. Him—crumpling the letter as if the words would disappear into the black hole of his fist. Me—needing him to say, "I love you. I haven't been unfaithful."

He never said it. When I finally summoned the strength to ask, big, fat, hot tears—bottled up all day—slipped from my eyes, slid down my face and washed away the words.

He held me until I stopped crying, until I murmured,
"Who would do this to us?"

"I don't know, Kate, but I'll sure as hell get to the bot-
tom of it."

The Ford Excursion behind me *beep-beep-beeps*, and
I realize the line has moved ahead at least five car
lengths. I'm still sitting in the same spot. I give a little
wave and pull up. I have to get a hold of myself.

To keep my mind from falling backward into the
sinkhole of doubt and fear, I focus on my breathing, the
way they teach us in yoga class.

Breathe in. Breathe out. Breathe in. Breathe out. Believe him. Or leave him. Believe him. Or leave him.

No! Stay present.

I drum my nails on the steering wheel. Outside my
window the sun is shining through barren trees; the
Volvo is still in front of me, the Ford Excursion still behind. Bundled-up children cling to their parents' hands
as they dash between cars toward the sidewalk ready for
a brisk walk home; the faint warble of the three-fifteen
school bell sounds, dismissing the bus riders—car riders leave at first bell.

The bell sounds remarkably similar to "Ode to Joy."
Oh. No, wait—that's my cell phone. Caitlin proba-

bly changed the ring again. It's one of her favorite pranks.

I grab my purse from the passenger seat. Fumble for the phone. Press Talk just before it switches to voice mail.

"Hello?"

"Are your bags packed?"

It's Alex.

"Noooooo—"

"Well get ready, I've booked us a room at The Breakers for the weekend of February seventh."

"That's only two weeks from now."

"Right. One of the weekends we all agreed on."

Breath in. Breath out. Breathe in. Breathe out.

"Kate? Are you there?"

"Yes. I—I just thought you'd choose one of the other options we agreed on."

"The Breakers is offering a fabulous spa package that weekend—you know, so close to Valentine's Day. We'd be crazy not to take advantage of it."

A knot the size of Texas moves into my stomach.

"You're still going, right?" she asks.

If I believe in my husband—if I trust him—I should have no reservations whatsoever. Just as I never had any doubt about going away with Rainey and Alex the nine previous years we've carried on this tradition.

"Of course I'm going. I have to let Corbin know." I hear myself saying the words, but they sound foreign. My heart's instinct is to protest, but I won't let it.

"This is going to be so much fun," says Alex.

More awkward silence crackles over the phone waves. I sense Alex searching for the words to ask what my problem is. But there is no problem. No siree. Not with my marriage. So I say, "I'm looking forward to it."

"Good. Me, too. I'm going to call Rainey now."

I hang up. Slide up two more spaces in the queue. Perform another rapid-fire cadence of steering wheel nail drumming, but it threatens to set my nerves on edge. So I turn on the radio to drown out the silence and pull from my purse the paint chips I selected today for the living room.

Five shades of beige for Corbin. One perfect blood-red sample called Scarlett O'Hara for me. He'll never go for it, but *I* like it. I fan them out as if I'm ready for a hand of six-card draw, study the subtle differences of the beiges, and absently sing along with the radio until it registers that Toni Braxton is wailing about the sadness of the word goodbye and having no joy in her life after her man walked out the door.

"Unbreak My Heart."

Uggggggggh. I used to love that song.

I swat at the radio as if it's a hornet about to sting me. The paint chips fly, but the scan button lands on a classic rock station playing a gritty guitar riff. A song I don't recognize.

Perfect.

I ease the car forward. Now, I can see the children waiting on the covered walkway. I bend down and retrieve the color chips.

Beige.

Beige.

Beige.

Scarlett O'Hara. Nope. He'll *never* go for it, despite how he always says, "You're the designer. Work your magic."

He always comes back to beige. And I say, "If you want it to remain the same, then why are we bothering?"

He says, "No, go ahead. We need a change."

I end up giving him the same old same old we've had since I began decorating our house twenty years ago.

Twenty years of beige.

Oh, dear God, I thought it was what he wanted.

Armed with a cocktail, Corbin's partner, Dave Sanders, answers his front door and greets us with a hearty, "Heeeeeey. It's the Hennesseys. Come in."

He takes our coats, slaps Corbin on the back, then pulls me into a tight bear hug, pressing his short, chubby body to mine in a way that makes me squirm. "Kate, you're gorgeous, as always."

His breath reeks of Scotch. Before I can break away, his free hand slithers down my back until he cups my bottom and gives it a little squeeze.

I draw in a sharp breath. *What the*—? I try to pull away, but he holds on to me, staring down at my breasts.

"What are you—about a B cup? My brother can give you a nice set of Ds and then you'd be just about the perfect woman."

I can't believe he just said that.

"Stop it." I push away from him, and a wave of Scotch splashes down the back of my silk blouse.

He laughs.

I dart a quick glance at his wife, Peg, and Corbin, who are finishing an air-kiss greeting, oblivious to Dave's unconscionable antics.

Dave's moved on into the high-ceilinged living room. I'm left pondering that surely he didn't mean it the way I'm imagining he did. In all the years I've known him, he's had a certain reputation as a ladies' man that's escalated to cheating louse as the practice became more successful, but that's between him and Peg. Except for a few off-color remarks about my inadequate boobs, he's never made a pass at me.

Tonight, he's obviously soused. Short of causing a scene, I can do nothing but stand there with the sick feeling of having been violated, and greet Peg, who offers me the same glassy-eyed air kiss she gave my husband.

"*Haaaaaai, huuuuuun,*" she slurs, the unmistakable smell of gin on her breath, the dregs of a drink in the glass she holds. The ice cubes clink as she steps back, a little unsteady on her feet, and brushes a wisp of short red hair off her pale forehead.

All this and it's only six-thirty.

It could be a very long night, except that I've got a theory. One of Corbin's partners, Mac or Dave, sent the letter. They *have* to be the culprits. The timing is just too coincidental: The envelope arrived yesterday. The dinner party's tonight. *Hello?*

These forty-something men who play doctor have

never outgrown their hazing, frat-boy mentality. My husband is the worst. He had Mac's brand-new Cadillac towed out of the parking lot to make him think it was stolen. Last year, when Dave turned forty-five, Corbin hired a stripper to come into the office and pose as a patient—feeding Dave's obsession with big boobs.

Tonight, I sense my otherwise upright, straitlaced husband, with his Jaguar and season subscription to the opera, is about to get the mother of all paybacks.

They're going to laugh about it at dinner. Make a big joke out of it.

Gotcha, Corb!

Well, I can take a joke as well as the next person. I don't know if Corbin's going to be so forgiving because this really pushes the bounds of bad taste. Will it be enough to curtail these monthly dinner parties?

Oh, wouldn't *that* be a shame.

I'd much rather it be a joke than to go on worrying and wondering....

We follow Peg into the living room where Dave holds out a Scotch on the rocks for Corbin and a glass of Chardonnay for me. I can't meet Dave's gaze. So I'm glad when the doorbell rings again.

Dave and Peg answer the door together. A moment

later they usher in Joan and Mac McCracken. I wonder if Dave gave Joan the same heinie-fondling, boob-assessing welcome he gave me?

If he did, it would make it less personal, but I'm certainly not going to say, "Hi, Joan. Did Dave grab your ass, too?"

What I'm going to do later is tell Corbin. Let him take care of it. I'm *not* getting breast implants. So Corbin can tell Dave *not* to mention it again. Not funny the first fifteen times he said it. Now, he's just running it into the ground.

Let's see if Corbin thinks this is as funny as his buddy's other misdeeds.

Actually, I need to give Corbin some credit. Funny is not the appropriate word. When he's regaled me with tales of his partners' libidinous exploits it's been more out of a sense of horror than amusement. It started after we bumped into Mac out with a woman-child who looked barely legal. Obviously a date. Joan was in Tuscany for the month. Alone. Well, presumably alone—who knows?

Peg, Joan and I aren't close enough to share intimate details like that. Even if I don't like them very much, I have to admit they're not stupid women. They have to know their husbands. How could they not? I don't understand how they can stay with men they know are unfaithful—turn the other cheek and jet off to Europe until the latest bimbette has lost her sheen.

I've always appreciated Corbin's honesty. After seeing Mac—God, it was before Caitlin was born—Corbin opened up to me. I hated hearing the dirty details, but it made me feel closer to my husband that he would share how much Dave's and Mac's dalliances bothered him. As close as they are, he said it was the one area in which he couldn't relate to them, said it disappointed him that they could look their wives in the eyes and lie.

I cling to that thought and believe in my husband.

Bring on the joke.

I can take it.

CHAPTER 3

There was no joke.

Nor a punch line.

Only the slow-dawning realization that Mac and Dave weren't the culprits. Someone else sent the letter.

Some unknown person, who, for some unknown reason, decided she—or he—and it could very well be a he, let's not jump to conclusions—wanted to mess with the solidarity of the Hennessey marriage.

So here I stand the morning after, in the kitchen, squeezing orange juice for Corbin's and Caitlin's breakfast, pondering *who* and *why* and trying to act as if I haven't a care in the world.

I've never been a good actress. I'm tired and cranky because I lay awake most of last night listening to Corbin snore.

The orange slips off the juicer, and my hand lands

in the sticky, pulpy mess. Oh for God's sake. It's mornings like this I wish I could pull a carton of OJ from the refrigerator. But I won't. I've always taken pride in giving my family the best. I rinse and dry my hand, return to the half-dozen orange halves on the cutting board.

I'm just tired. Everything always seems worse when I'm tired.

"Corbin?"

He's sitting at the table, a bowl of oatmeal in front of him, engrossed in the newspaper. He doesn't look up from the business section. A prickle of irritation spirals through my veins, and I'm tempted to throw a spent orange hull at his paper fortress. Instead, I toss the peel into the sink.

"Do you want to hear something funny?" I ask.

"Mmm…" He folds the paper in half then over again. Still reading, he reaches for a piece of toast on a plate next to his cereal. Absently, he takes a bite.

I pick up another orange half. "I thought Dave and Mac were the ones who wrote the letter."

He lowers the paper and looks at me as if I'm an idiot.

I shrug. "I thought they were playing a joke."

He frowns. "A damn lousy joke. They wouldn't do something like that. " He sounds irritated, defensive, as if he'd never considered them suspect. The crease between his brows deepens, and he retreats behind his newspaper. I hate the way he shuts down in the middle of a conversation. Because I always have plenty left to say.

"Yes, Corbin, it *is* a lousy thing to do. Do you have any idea who did it?"

"Kate." It's more of a sigh than a word. He lays the business section on the table, checks his watch, stands. "Just let it go. Bottom line is I love you. I love our family. I'm not going to do anything to screw up what we have." He walks over and puts his arms around me. "The only way the letter matters is if we let it matter. So let it go."

I sink into him. His arms feel so right around me. This is my place. But reservation seeps in and rakes its cold, bony fingers over every inch of my body, leaving me breathless and slightly nauseated. He's right, though. I'm sure whoever did this wants a reaction just like the elementary school bully wanted attention. The question is, whose attention does this bully want?

"You think if we ignore it, it will simply go away?"

"Will who go away, Mommy?" Caitlin walks into the kitchen dressed for school. She hesitates in front of her seat at the table and looks at Corbin and me.

He releases me and returns to the table.

"No one, sweetie. Daddy and I were just talking about—"

"No one of any consequence." Corbin tickles Caitlin. "So don't you worry your pretty little head over it."

Her laughter crescendos into high-pitched screams, and he draws her into a snuggly Daddy-hug that melts my heart because it speaks louder than all the words he could utter to convince me of his dedication.

I shove the orange down on the marble head of the electric appliance. The machine growls as it pulverizes the fruit. Wouldn't it be nice if I could purge myself of doubt the way the juicer forces the pulp from the orange?

"What's consequence?" Caitlin asks, a spoonful of oatmeal poised in front of her mouth.

"A person of no consequence is someone of no importance," says Corbin. "Someone who doesn't matter."

I pour the juice into glasses. "A consequence is also the result of your actions. You do something bad, you suffer the consequence."

The words slip out before I realize the implication. My cheeks burn.

Corbin cuts his gaze to me and hesitates before he scrapes the last bite of oatmeal from his bowl. I carry two glasses of juice to the table and set one in front of Caitlin. I hold the other until my husband looks me in the eye again.

Resolve gleams in his clear azure eyes. A determination that dictates conversation about the letter is over. Okay. If he can still look me in the eye, what else do I need to make myself feel better?

So that's it.

I can believe him, or I can leave him.

I believe him.

He reaches up, takes the glass, sips it and raises it toward me with a slight nod. "Thank you."

He picks up the paper again. He looks good in his sapphire-blue shirt and yellow tie. The shirt matches his eyes, which are in crisp contrast to his nearly black hair. For a moment I'm transported back to my freshman year at the University of Florida, when we first met. I was working my way through school. He was the carefree frat boy. The cocky rich kid who had the world at his feet. My family is close, but we're of simple means. Yet out of all the debutantes and sorority girls, the moneyed coeds with deep Southern roots and families with even deeper pockets, Corbin chose me. He used to say, *Money can't buy class, Kate. Either you're born with it or you're not.* Every single day of our twenty-year marriage, I've done my best to make sure he didn't live to regret his choice.

As I pull out my chair to take my place at the table with my coffee, I spy the paint chips on the windowsill and pick them up.

"I talked to Alex yesterday," I say as I shuffle through the colors. "It's time for our annual getaway. But I don't know...."

He lowers the paper. "This early?"

"Well, that's just it. She and Rainey have their hearts set on this spa weekend down at the Breakers. It's in two weeks." I shake my head.

"What's the date?"

"February seventh, but it's too soon. Not enough notice. I'll tell them to go ahead without me. Maybe the girls and I can plan a trip later this year, closer to our birthdays."

He shrugs. "It should be fine. I'm on call this weekend. That means Mac or Dave will be on the weekend you're away. I'm sure your mother will help out if there's an emergency."

Emergency? What does he expect to happen?

The words from the letter telegraph in my brain:

Ask your husband what he's been doing all those nights he claimed to be at the hospital.

No.

Stop it. I will not keep going there. Am I really going to let some unknown person control my relationship with my husband? A man I've known for twenty years?

"I don't want you to go, Mommy." Caitlin frowns up at me, her blond brows knit into a single line across her smooth forehead.

Corbin reaches out and takes my hand. The paint chips scatter on the table.

"No, Caitlin, your mommy deserves to do this for herself. Sometimes we forget that she never gets a break."

He draws my hand to his lips, kisses my knuckles. The gesture is so sweet, so tender. My eyes mist. I close them until I'm able to swallow the lump in my throat.

To keep my mind on the positive, I say, "Take a look at these colors." I nudge the samples toward him. "I'd like to get the living room painted before I go."

He picks up the sport section and scrutinizes a photo of an Orlando Magic player scoring the winning point at a recent game. "Whatever you want. You're the one with good taste."

I scoot the Scarlett O'Hara chip toward him. "Okay, then this one."

He peers over the top corner of the paper and laughs. "Not in my house. This belongs in a bordello. Besides, isn't red supposed to excite people? I need to relax when I get home."

If he hadn't been so darn sweet just a short moment ago, I'd argue Scarlett O'Hara's case. For now, she can wait.

"I'll be home after the game tonight. Are you sure you and Caitlin don't want to come?"

I shake my head.

"Awwwwww, Mommy. I want to go."

"No, you were too hard to wake up this morning and you have school tomorrow. Another time. A weekend game, perhaps."

Corbin stands, kisses Caitlin on the top of her head. "Come to think of it, I'll be pretty late. After the game, there's a reception at Harvey's Bistro for the new general manager. I need to put in an appearance. New management could decide on a new team physician. I need to stake our claim."

I steel myself against the queer swirling sensation in my gut. Everything is fine. He will go to his game. I will go to Palm Beach.

Everything is fine.

Alex and Rainey are surveying the loot from our shopping spree and settling into our luxury suite at the Breakers as I punch numbers on my cell phone. It's only seven-thirty. Our dinner reservation is for eight, and I want to call home and say goodnight to Caitlin before it gets much later.

The phone rings. I settle back against the padded headboard waiting for someone to answer, watching Rainey model a new dress she bought in a shop on Worth Avenue.

Rainey twirls. Alex gives the thumbs-up sign. She doesn't have kids or a husband—which, she says, is a good thing, given the fact she can't even hold together a relationship with her mother. They haven't spoken in ten years. That's sad. I can't imagine what I'd do without my mother, but it's Alex's life. She says she's perfectly happy having only to check in with her law office's answering service.

Rainey's only child, Ben, will graduate from high

school in May. He probably won't realize she's gone for the weekend until she gets back and tries to torture him with photographs.

Rainey's a pro when it comes to cameras. She's by far the most creative of the three of us. She's argued that point with me on more than one occasion, giving me credit for my "decorating flair." But my *panache*, as she calls it, does not hold a candle to what Rainey can create with a lump of clay and the artistic equivalent of a funky manicure set. She's amazing. By default—and because Alex and I didn't even bother to bring a camera—she's the official photographer of the tenth annual girls' getaway.

She snaps a shot of me with the phone pressed to my ear. I'm counting the rings on the other end of the line. Seven…eight… A couple more and the answering machine will kick in, but in the nick of time Caitlin picks up the receiver. Her little voice sings, "Hello, Hennessey residence."

"Hi, sweetie."

"Mommy! When are you coming home? I miss you."

"Pumpkin, I haven't been gone twenty-four hours. How can you miss me already?"

"I just do. Don't you miss me?"

"Of course I do, but I'm having fun, too. We went shopping today and had our nails done. We just checked into our room."

"Did you get me a surprise?"

"I sure did."

"What color did you get your nails painted?"

"Natural."

"Just like always. When you get home will you paint my nails pink?"

"I will. Maybe I'll even find a special bottle of pretty pink polish to bring home to you."

"Ohhhhhhhh! Don't forget, okay?"

"All right, sweetie. Can you put Daddy on the phone for a minute?"

"No."

No? My heart kicks against my breastbone, and I sit up and scoot to the edge of the bed. "Why not?"

"He's sleeping."

What? In all the time I've known this man, he's never napped. "What's wrong? Is he okay?"

"I think so."

A bad feeling creeps into my veins. Caitlin isn't a baby, of course, but if he's sick he should've called my mother to come help, rather than leaving her to fend for herself while he slept. I turn toward the window. It's dark outside.

"How long has he been asleep?"

"I dunno."

"Have you had dinner?"

"No, and I'm hungry."

I stand up. It's nearly bedtime. I knew this trip was a bad idea.

"Take the phone into him and tell him Mommy wants to talk to him."

Rainey and Alex have stopped their shopping show-and-tell and are staring at me.

"He'll get mad. Just like you're mad."

I take a deep breath and soften my tone. "I'm not mad, honey. I'm concerned about Daddy. And you. I'm sorry if I sounded angry."

I walk into the living room, away from my audience. "Honey, put him on the phone, and then I'll talk to you again before I hang up. Okay?"

A few moments later, a groggy voice croaks, "Yeah? Doctor Hennessey."

"Corbin, it's me. What's wrong?"

He grunts. I picture him sitting up, swinging his legs over the edge of the bed and running his hand over his eyes and through his hair in one motion. "Oh, Kate. It's you." His voice is breathy. "I thought it was the hospital. Oh God... I didn't mean to sleep so long. I just... passed out."

Passed out? I quell the mother tiger urge to tear into him. You don't *pass out* when you're taking care of a child. Staring at the maroon-velvet-striped wallpaper, I silently count to ten and give him the benefit of the doubt. "Are you sick?"

"No. I was...tired." His voice tightens on the last word. "I'm entitled to take a nap every once in a while."

"I'm not saying you aren't. But it's seven-thirty, and your daughter hasn't even eaten dinner. When you're caring for a six-year-old, *entitlement* gets put on hold for the weekend."

He snorts.

The urge to ask if I need to come home wraps around me like a scratchy wool blanket begging me to throw it off my shoulders and onto the table. But I draw it tightly around me and endure the itch.

"It's only two days. Come on, you can handle it."

The long, drawn-out silence underscores every mile that stretches between us, until I can't stand it anymore.

"Corbin, she's only six. If you have to check out, or

pass out or whatever you did, take her to my mother's house so someone's looking after her, okay?"

"Oh, for God's sake—" He draws in a heavy breath. Lets it out. "You're right. You're always right, Kate. I'd better get in there and start cooking. Have fun shopping. Goodbye."

"Don't forget the—" click "—lasagna in the refrigerator."

I look at my phone. Call ended.

He hung up on me.

Oh! Irritation simmers in the pit of my stomach, threatening to rage into a full boil. I squeeze the phone until my knuckles turn white and stare at it as if it will channel all my anger back to my husband and reach out and slap him. *What* is his problem?

A vision of my daughter's face pops into my mind. We didn't even get to say good-night. I start to call home again—

"Everything all right?" Alex asks.

I jump and turn toward her in one quick, jerky motion, and snap the phone closed. Alex is standing in the middle of the living-room floor, hands on her hips. From the concerned look on her face, I'm certain she heard every word of my conversation. Through the bedroom doorway, I see Rainey seated at the dressing table, touching up her makeup, watching me in the mirror.

Heat floods my cheeks. I feel like an idiot.

"Everything's fine." I grab my purse off the coffee table and shove the phone inside. "We'd better go or we'll miss our reservation."

Out in the hall the air is cool and carries that old, upscale hotel smell of brass polish and carpet shampoo. Our suite is at the end of the corridor. Three doors down a fortyish man and twenty-something brunette step into the hallway. They don't see me. Or maybe they do, but they don't care. He closes the door, draws her to him in a feverish kiss. I watch them shamelessly. His hands skim her slim body, wind their way around to her derriere where they linger, kneading and pulling her into him for the duration of the kiss.

They laugh, kiss again, coo at each other, and finally walk away, arms entwined, past the other rooms that stretch down the passage like twin rows of soldiers standing at attention, guarding tawdry secrets. Shiny knobs and numbered plates glint in the dim light, but betray nothing of the lovers who grace these halls.

A voice deep inside me prods and pokes me in vulnerable places. "You know what's going on, Kate. *You know*. Now you have to decide if you're going to turn the other cheek or start opening some doors."

We get back to the hotel before midnight. I'm remarkably relaxed. Equalized, you might say. Amazing the miracles worked by good friends, a delicious meal and more than a few glasses of Chardonnay.

Ahh… Medicine to soothe the weary soul.

I fall onto the overstuffed, floral sofa, let my head loll back into the cushion and close my eyes for a minute.

"This is exactly what I needed," Rainey says as she toes out of her sandals. "It's good for us to get away. It makes our men miss us. And appreciate us."

I nod and look at Alex. I see two of her and blink until the images meld into one. My head is spinning. I put my hand on my forehead to make it stop.

I never drink this much. But a girl's gotta do what a girl's gotta do. It was either anesthe…a—nes—the—tize—phewwww, say that after several glasses of wine. Anyhow, it was either numb myself or cry in my soup and ruin everyone's dinner. That wouldn't have been very nice. Especially given that the girls didn't even ask about my phone call. Wise women. I like that about them. Good friends. They have a sixth sense that tells them when to prod and when to leave it alone.

Instead, we talk about tomorrow's plans—more shopping, the beach, a massage. Then Rainey goes off on her usual hour-long tirade about how her husband pays no attention to her, which I suspect may have been meant as a segue for me to jump in and talk about my phone spat with Corbin, but I don't cross the threshold. Uh-uh. Not going there. In fact, that little voice that keeps nagging me saying—"You know what he's doing, Kate. You know."—I tell it to shut up.

And then Alex gives Rainey her standard logic against Rainey's staying with a man who won't make love to her. "Did you get married to become a nun?" She asked her that.

It's kinda funny if you think about it.

Well, naaaa, really it's not. It kinda sucks, actually. At least Corbin and I still do it. Well, we used to. It's been a while. But I don't want to talk about it. So anyway, after Alex goes off, Rainey starts with her defense of the ups and downs of holy matrimony.

All this in the span of two bottles of wine. I couldn't get a word in if I wanted to. All I do is sit, sip and go along for the ride.

Now, we're back at the hotel, and they're all talked out. It's a good thing, because my head hurts.

Alex stands up and stretches. "It's way past my bedtime. I'm calling it a night."

"I'm not far behind you," says Rainey. "Who wants the bathroom first?"

The two disappear into the bedroom to sort it out. Inertia takes hold of me, and tugs me into a prone position on the couch. Maybe closing my eyes will make the dizziness go away.

Yeahhhhh…that's better… Except that all I can see in my mind's eye is the long double row of doors outside in the hotel hallway and that damned kissing couple a few rooms down. And this time when the man draws back from the embrace, it's…Corbin who's grinding himself into the brunette.

I sit up too fast, which causes my already pounding head to split. I swallow against a wave of nausea.

My purse is on the coffee table, and I fish out my cell phone, letting my PDA, lipsticks and receipts fall where they may.

Dialing my home number, I pay no attention to the little voice that warns me that it's after midnight. *Shut up! Weren't you just saying, "You know. You know." Well, I've had enough of you. Shut up.*

The line rings twice before a young woman answers.

"Hennessey residence."

I'm jolted sober. A coppery taste fills my already dry mouth and bile burns the back of my throat.

"This is Kate Hennessey. May I speak to Corbin, please?"

My words are short and enunciated. Much too polite for this woman who's in my house, answering my phone. I should call her a home-wrecking bitch-slut. Because that's what she is—

"Hi, Mrs. Hennessey. This is Jenny Long. Dr. Hennessey had an emergency at the hospital and called me about an hour ago to come in and stay with Caitlin."

"Oh."

My hand flies to my mouth in an automatic reflex. This young woman, whom I nearly called a home-wrecking bitch-slut, is, in fact, the college girl we call when we need an overnight sitter and my mother's not available. Why did Corbin call her and not my mother?

What about Dave and Mac? One of the moron twins was supposed to be on call this weekend. Why is Corbin at the hospital instead of them?

Ask your husband what he's been doing all those nights he claimed to be at the hospital.

A scream blooms low in my belly and expands, threatening to overpower me. Somehow I manage to ask in a civilized tone, "Hi, Jenny, when did Corbin say he'd be home?"

"He wasn't sure. He said he might be late—or early, depending on how you look at it. He said if he wasn't home by the time Caitlin woke up, I should feed her."

I can't breathe and the walls start to close in on me. Not only is the room spinning, but now the floor is dropping out from under me. "Thanks, Jenny." I don't know where my voice comes from, but it catches me like a safety net, and I'm grateful for it.

"Sure, Mrs. Hennessey. If it's urgent, you can always page him or phone him at the hospital."

"Yes, thanks, I'll do that."

I hang up the phone, sick with dread, knowing what

I have to do. The longer I put off the call, the harder it'll be to place. I'm not going to call his cell phone because if he's not where he's supposed to be, he'll know he's caught. But if I call the hospital and he's there, I can tell him I felt bad about the way we left things when we spoke earlier, tell him I love him and want to end the night on a better note.

Yes, that's it.

I pull up the numbers stored in my phone and page through the list until I come to Winter Park Hospital. I hit the automatic dial key. My heart pounds so hard I feel faint.

The automated attendant picks up, and I press O. "Operator, how may I direct your call?"

I can barely speak, but I manage. "This is Kate Hennessey, Dr. Hennessey's wife. Would you page him, please?"

I suck in a breath.

"Sure. Hold please."

A moment later she comes back on the line. "I'm sorry, Mrs. Hennessey, Dr. Hennessey isn't here this evening."

Her words are a white-hot jolt, an arrow shot straight

through the bull's-eye of my heart, confirming every in-kling of doubt I've had for the past three weeks.

Ask your husband what he's been doing all those nights he claimed to be at the hospital.

No!
Believe him or leave him.
"I believe he was called in on an emergency. Could you check one more time, please? It's urgent."

I'm shaking. Not a little quiver, but huge quaking shudders racking my entire body. I hold on the line, feeling small and sure that the operator knows how pathetically insecure I am. Yet, I have the mental clarity to wonder what I'm going to say to him if somehow, miraculously, Corbin's voice comes on the line.

But deep down I know my husband's not at the hospital. I have no idea where he is or who he's with.

"Mrs. Hennessey, I spoke with the charge nurse and she says Dr. Hennessey hasn't been in all evening. Have you tried paging him?"

No. I don't want to talk to him. I want to know if he's where he told the sitter he'd be. "That's a great idea."

"May I take a message in case he comes in?"

I'm slipping, melting from the inside out.

"No, thank you. I'm out of town. I must have misunderstood his schedule for this evening."

"Well then, have a good night."

CHAPTER 4

Picture Thelma and Louise chauffeured by Lorena Bobbitt. That's what we look like as we drive back to Orlando from Palm Beach.

We check out of the Breakers at two o'clock in the morning after Rainey and Alex discover me collapsed in an inconsolable, sobbing heap.

I don't want Rainey and Alex to leave because of me, and I'm perfectly prepared to rent a car and drive myself. They won't have any part of staying.

"Whether we come with you or not, the weekend is ruined," says Alex.

"I'm sorry. I shouldn't have come in the first place."

"No, that's not what I meant, Kate." She takes me by the shoulders and forces me to look at her. "I know I speak for Rainey, too, when I say we can't stay here and let you go home to this situation alone. You're in no condition to drive. Besides, we want to be with you when you catch the bastard with his pants down."

I dissolve all over again.

Rainey murmurs, "Shut up. You're making it worse." She sits down next to me on the couch and hugs me. "It's going to be okay, Kate. You're a strong lady. You'll be fine. Until you can stand on your own, we're here for you."

I try to sit up and realize snot is stringing from my nose. I try to wipe it away with the back of my hand. Alex hands me a tissue.

"God, I'm ruining everything—"

"You're not," says Alex. "We'll reschedule for another time. Right now, we have more important matters to tend to."

Rainey sits with me in the backseat and every so often she reaches out and squeezes my hand. The drive from Palm Beach is taking an eternity, as if I'm stuck in a surreal time warp. Rainey gave me a Valium before we left. I'm sure that's why everything has a soft-focus, blunted feel. It would be good if we were stuck in a time warp. I wouldn't have to face him.

Just when I've convinced myself this is a bad dream that will be over soon, Alex hisses something like,

"That no-good, dirty, lying, son of a bitch," and I'm jolted back to the here and now.

As Alex's black Mercedes rolls over the endless black ribbon of Florida Turnpike, all I can think of is how Corbin lied to me.

To us.

To our family.

My forehead is pressed to the cool window. The car is eerily silent except for the rhythmic *wrrrrrrrr* of car wheels spinning over flat highway. Alex doesn't turn on the radio. We all settle into a companionable silence. The headlights shining across the median hurt my eyes. I squint as another car speeds by. Thank goodness there's not much traffic at this hour.

My eyes feel heavy, threaten to close. I'm so sleepy, but I don't want to sleep, because if I do, the next time I open my eyes we'll be back in Orlando. If I can only stay awake… It's the Valium—and the wine and the hour—tempting me to drift…off.

"Where did you get the Valium?" I ask, not lifting my head from the window.

"I have a good doctor."

This time I can't distinguish if my silent tears fall because of the way the words *good doctor* stab at my heart, or because I'm thankful to have these women in my life.

A while later I startle awake to the sound of Rainey's voice. "There could be a logical explanation."

They think I'm asleep. I was asleep. Damn it, how long did I sleep? I shift my head ever so slightly until I can see Alex's brown eyes looking at Rainey in the neon-green glow of the lighted rearview mirror.

My neck hurts, and I long to sit up and rub it, but I don't move because if I do they'll stop talking. I wait for one of them to say something, to reveal the *logical explanation* my life is depending on. There must be something obvious I've missed. Please, please enlighten me.

"Maybe he's truly been called out on an emergency."

Alex answers with dead silence. Her dark eyes look black as they alternately shift from the rearview mirror, to the road, back to the mirror. I get the creepy sensation that I'm stuck in a scene from a bizarre David Lynch movie. Especially when I hear Alex groan.

Or maybe it's me.

Being on this side of the truth feels a lot different than I imagined before I dared let my mind venture into the what-ifs of the dark, lonely place inhabited by scorned wives. Speculating on Corbin's infidelity was like standing atop a cliff overlooking a tumultuous ocean. Finding out is like falling headfirst and crashing into the waves and rocks below.

"Why doesn't she just call his cell phone?" Rainey says.

"No. That's the worst thing she could do. She was smart not to. If he's not at the hospital and she calls him on the cell he'll have time to concoct some cockama-mie story to cover his ass. This way, she can get some answers."

The unspoken words *good answers or bad answers* loom over me like henchmen.

Alex holds the steering wheel with her left hand and digs in her purse with the other until she pulls out her cell phone. She holds it up. "Rainey, take this and scroll through my phone numbers until you get Hal Washington."

The Mercedes swerves a little. It shimmies as Alex returns to her lane.

"Hey, watch out. Both hands on the wheel." Rainey takes the phone.

"That's why I'm asking you to find the number and dial it for me."

"Why are you calling this guy now? It's three-thirty in the morning."

"Believe me, Washington thrives at this hour."

"What is he, a vampire?"

"Close. He's a P.I. I'm going to get him to tail Corbin."

Rainey leans forward and wraps her arms around the passenger headrest. "Shouldn't you ask Kate if that's what she wants before you hire a detective on her behalf? I mean, it's a big deal. And it could be a little pricey."

"Washington owes me a favor. Actually, several, but who's counting? The sooner Kate knows for sure, the better."

I sit up. The crick in my neck screams. "A P.I. could also prove whether Corbin was innocent. Right?"

There's a beat of silence as Rainey's head whips around and Alex's eyes dart to find me in the rearview mirror. I'm not sure whether they're surprised that I'm awake and listening to their scheming, or dumbfounded that I still harbor hope. I rub my neck waiting for them to answer me.

"I suppose," says Alex. "Whatever he's up to, Washington will find out. So yes, if Corbin's taking a midnight flower-arranging class, Washington will let you know. Can I call him?"

The moment of truth. My stomach clenches. Do I really want to know? I'm not sure, but one thing I do know is I can't go on *not* knowing. "Sure."

Rainey lets go of the headrest and settles into the backseat. She punches in the phone number. "Here, it's ringing." She hands the phone to Alex.

I think Rainey and I are holding our breath in the silent seconds before Alex starts talking. I'm looking out the window again so I can't see her. We roll past a series of lighted billboards advertising the virtues of Yeehaw Junction, the turnpike exit before Kissimmee. We're twenty minutes or so outside of Orlando. My stomach accelerates from clenching to pitching as I realize the moment of truth is nearly staring me in the face.

What next? If I go home and he's not there, I'll have to explain to the babysitter why I'm back.

Oh God, she'll know.

I can't go to the hospital. It would be humiliating to walk in and ask if they know the whereabouts of my husband in the wee hours of a Saturday morning.

Alex holds the cell phone away from her. "Kate, can you meet with Hal at ten in the morning?"

"Okay."

"Good. Ten it is. My office. See you then."

I glance at my watch and realize that's only a few hours from now.

Alex hangs up and tosses the phone onto the passenger seat. "What do you want to do when we get into Orlando?"

Go to Disney World? Shop the designer outlet malls? Catch my husband in bed with another woman? Oh, the endless possibilities. "I don't know what I want to do. I just know what I can't do. I can't go home, and I can't go to the hospital."

Rainey pats my hand.

"But we need to see if Corbin's at home," says Alex. "Chances are—now bear with me, this is worst-case scenario, chances are if he's gone off with someone, he's not going to be back yet."

"I don't know," says Rainey. "Don't you think he'd try to sneak back in and get rid of the sitter before Caitlin wakes up? Because Caitlin will tell Mommy."

"That's a good point," says Alex. "It should be interesting to see if he tells you he brought in the sitter. Would be a good way to see if he's forthcoming with information. If he tells you up front, then maybe he'll have a logical explanation to go along with it."

I nod. A crazy mixture of hope and fear meld inside me.

"It'll be a good gauge to see what you're dealing with," Rainey says.

Alex steers the car off the turnpike, pays the toll and merges onto Interstate Four. "Okay, let's make a plan."

The house sleeps dark and quiet. Just as it should in the five o'clock Saturday morning dusk. The only thing out of place is the red Honda Civic parked in the driveway behind my garaged Lexus.

Jenny's car.

I love this house—its old-world Mediterranean charm, the overgrown live oak between us and the neighbor's that shelters us like protective arms, the rolling lawn that stretches to the street like green carpet.

Before we bought it, Corbin made such a production of showing me the place. "Close your eyes," he'd said before we turned onto Via Lugano. "Don't peek…. Okay, now open them. I found your dream house, Mrs. Hennessey."

"Stop and let me out," I say.

Rainey grabs my arm as if she fears I might jump out before Alex comes to a complete stop. "You're not going in there."

I shake my head. "I want to see if his car's in the garage."

"What?"

"Why?" They say in unison.

"That's the sitter's car, right?" Alex says. "Honey, he's not home."

I nod. I don't know why I want to check. I just have to see for myself that his car's not there. "Maybe he's home—"

"Is he sleeping with the babysitter?" Rainey narrows her eyes.

"Jenny?" The possibility jolts me. I hadn't even considered it. "No. No way. I thought that maybe…" Both of them are staring at me, patently horrified, as if they're afraid I'm going to do something to harm myself. "I don't know. Maybe he just got home?"

"If that's the case," says Alex, "then we'd better get out of here fast, because Jenny, or whatever her name is, will walk out any minute and blow our cover."

I fish in my purse for my keys. "Then pull down the street a little. I'm going to let myself in the side garage door and have a peek."

I hop out of the car, take three steps and my foot lands on a small pebble in the street. I lose my balance and turn my ankle.

It dawns on me that I'm still wearing the little black dress and strappy sandals I wore to dinner last night. God, that seems like aeons ago. Why didn't I change clothes before we left? Come to think of it, I hope Alex and Rainey got my suitcase, because I have no recollection of packing it or putting it in the car.

My ankle throbs, but I ignore it and glance up and down the street looking for any neighbors who might be lurking in the predawn darkness. The air smells of winter and has that cold, dewy quality that rains on Florida in the middle of the night instead of blanketing the ground with frost. I shiver.

All I can see is the glowing red taillights of Alex's car parked in the street two houses down. If the neighbors see me getting out of a strange car dressed like this at this hour, it will look bad. When they hear that Corbin and I are divorcing, they're going to think *I'm* the one who cheated.

Anger merges with despair, and tears brim at the thought of—*divorce*. It's like a well-landed punch to the gut. I want to throw myself down on the carpet of grass and bawl, but instead, I limp as fast as I can—ouch, my ankle really hurts—up the driveway to the garage door on the side of the house.

I must be in more of a stupor than I realize, because it's only after the burglar alarm blares that I remember the only door you can enter without setting off the system is the front door.

"Oh shit!"

My dog, Jack, is barking and throwing himself against the door so hard, I'm afraid he'll break through. In a matter of seconds, the neighbors are going to look out to see what the racket's about, and the police are going to arrive to find me breaking into my own house.

I do what any person in this situation with half a brain would do—I run.

Excruciating pain be damned, I run as fast as I can to Alex's car, turning the same ankle twice more before I jump in, and we speed away like criminals.

"What the hell happened back there?" Alex says.

I collapse into the backseat. "I forgot about the alarm system."

Despite the chilly February morning air, I've broken a sweat. I wipe away the moisture and reach down and rub my ankle. It's already swollen to twice its normal size.

Caitlin is going to be so scared. And Jenny—she'll be able to turn off the alarm since she turned it on— same code, but will she know the password? Will she call Corbin? Does she even know how to get in touch with Corbin? She thinks he's at the hospital.

When we're a safe distance away from my neighborhood, I hear police sirens wail in the distance. I don't know whether to laugh or cry.

"Are you okay?" Rainey asks.

"I forgot how to sprint in four-inch heels."

"Is it broken? Do you need to get it checked?"

"No." I unbuckle the strap and the pain shoots all the way up my calf. "If I did, at least I'd have a valid excuse for going to the hospital."

"So let's go." Alex coasts to a stop at the intersection of Aloma and Lakemont. The hospital is just past the intersection on the east side of Aloma.

"No! He's not there. What am I supposed to say when the nurses start asking questions? *How'd you sprain your ankle, Mrs. Hennessey?* I was running away after I set off the alarm system at my own house. *Where's your husband tonight, Mrs. Hennessey?* I don't know. He said he was going to be here tonight, I was hoping you might have seen him."

"So his car wasn't in the garage?" Rainey says.

I shake my head. "Just mine."

"It wasn't a bad idea to double-check," says Alex. "In fact, where's the doctor's parking lot? Let's drive by just in case."

"It's right next to the entrance, but you can't get in

because you need a card to access the gate. Security's on duty 24-7. Even if we tried to walk in they're going to ask questions."

Besides, I can tell by the way my entire leg throbs that I'm not fit to walk any great distance. "Isn't it a good sign if you have pain? Doesn't it mean the bone's not broken?"

"I think so," says Rainey.

Hmm… Imagine that. Pain, a good thing.

"I'm still going to swing around that way and see what we can see."

She does, and just as I predict, we see nothing. Alex drives into the hospital's visitor parking lot and pulls into one of the spaces.

"What are you doing?" I sit up straight. "I said I'm not going in there."

She kills the engine, unbuckles her seat belt then turns around to look at me. "Are you sure you're okay?"

"It depends on what you're asking. My ankle's fine— or I'm sure it will be. As for the rest of me—I'll have to get back to you."

Rainey pats her lap. "Put your foot up here."

I slant her a dubious glance.

"Come on." From the look on her face, I'm afraid

she's going to reach down and lift up my leg herself if I don't comply. "You need to elevate it. And you really should put some ice on it. Alex, can we go somewhere and get her some ice? And an Ace bandage, too."

"Sure, but first, Kate, what's the number for the hospital?"

"Why?" I ask, settling my foot on top of the jacket Rainey's balled up and set on her lap.

"Since we're here, we might as well double-check that he didn't show up after all."

I'm flooded by the realization of what a catch-22 this phone call is. If she phones and he's not in, I'm screwed because my husband's not where he said he'd be. If she calls and he's there, I've ruined the weekend.

I feel very strange having Alex drive me halfway across Florida, while I sit in the backseat as if she's my own private chauffeur. Now I'm sitting here in the hospital parking with my foot propped in Rainey's lap as if I'm the Queen of Sheba. We're the best of friends, but this goes above and beyond. What they've done for me since we left Palm Beach has broken the outer bounds of friendship. My eyes flood again, and I pull out my cell from my purse and hand it to Alex. "The number's stored. Use my phone to call."

She takes it. "No. I'll use mine. Just in case they track the incoming calls. I wouldn't want your name flashing on their screen."

An ambulance wails and a few seconds later pulls into the emergency entrance that's right across from the visitors' parking lot.

Alex turns around and faces forward to make the call.

"Yes, hello, may I speak to Doctor Corbin Hennessey, please? ... Certainly."

There's a pause and we all seem to be holding our breaths waiting for the answer.

"Oh right, yes, this is the pharmacist at Walgreens drugstore. I have a question about a prescription Dr. Hennessey wrote tonight... I'd prefer to hold rather than leaving my number. The customer's waiting...."

Alex glances at us, grimaces and rolls her eyes, then turns around again.

I'm watching the paramedics unload their emergency patient from the back of the ambulance. A team of nurses and a doctor I don't recognize meet them at the entrance. Their routine is as well choreographed as a difficult dance.

"No, that's not a good idea," Alex says into the phone. "You see, we're...ummmm... We're having trouble with our phone system. We can dial out but no one can dial in. That's why I'd prefer to hold… Certainly, I'll hold."

Alex glances back at Rainey and me and shrugs. She covers the receiver with her hand and whispers, "They're paging him—Oh, right, yes, I'm here…." Alex grips the steering wheel with her free hand. "Oh, yes, I see. He hasn't been in all weekend."

CHAPTER 5

Alex and Rainey deliver me home at seven o'clock on Sunday night. The ever-dutiful wife is right on time. When we pull in, there are no extra cars in the driveway. If I open the side garage door, this time I will not set off the alarm and will, in fact, find Corbin's car parked next to mine where it should be.

Alex pops the trunk. Both she and Rainey get out to help with my suitcase.

"Are you sure you're all right?" The streetlight casts a halo on Rainey's blond curly hair. She looks like an angel of mercy.

"I'll be fine." Even though I don't feel fine.

I wish she hadn't asked me because I was doing fine until she brought it up. I think she realizes it because she and Alex stand there for a couple of beats not saying anything. Alex picks up my suitcase and carries it to the front porch.

The big houses on my street look different bathed in the darkening twilight glow. It's a vignette I've seen hundreds of times over the twelve years we've lived here, but tonight it looks different.

I can't put my finger on what's changed. The old-fashioned street lamps glow, same as always. A few porch lights are lit. White smoke wafts from chimneys. It's as if I've been away for a very long time and am seeing the mundane with new eyes. How is it that you can look at something every day for years and not really see it?

It hits me that if Corbin and I get a divorce we'll have to sell the house, because that's what divorced people do. Maybe it wouldn't be such a bad thing. Could I live in that house with those beige walls without him?

Of course not. I'd have to paint them Scarlett O'Hara red. Maybe redecorate the living room in that Moroccan theme that's in my new *Architectural Digest*.

"Call me tomorrow and let me know how everything goes, okay?" says Rainey. "Or call me tonight after you put Caitlin to bed if you need to talk."

The click of Alex's heels on the pavers sounds overly loud as she rejoins us.

"Are you sure you don't want us to go in with you?"

She's standing there—all five foot eleven of her—with her hands fisted on her slim hips looking as though she wants to punch Corbin.

"Wouldn't we be a formidable sight?" I say. "The scorned wife with her angry posse come to lynch the cheating bastard husband. Corbin wouldn't know what hit him."

I try to laugh, but my voice cracks.

On good days my husband doesn't understand the female need to bond. If he caught sight of us now—the mood we're in—I'm sure he'd run for the hills without pausing to ask questions. As much as I dread walking this path alone, I must.

I shake my head.

Rainey and Alex exchange a glance.

"Then we're going to take off, okay?" says Alex. "Call us if you need anything. I can be here in a jiff."

I nod.

We hug.

They get in the car.

I stand in the driveway and watch the car's taillights grow smaller, finally rounding the corner and disappearing from sight.

It's cold outside. I pull my jacket closer around my

neck. This was supposed to be the trip that capped off the last year of our thirties. Oh God, I hope it's not an omen of what's to come as I cross the midlife threshold.

I'm going to be forty and divorced. After twenty years of marriage, I've given half my life to this man—and it comes to this?

This does not bode well.

Does divorce mean half my life is gone? Is it all erased with the signing of papers? Written off like a bad investment?

The voice of reason tries to slam a mental door on the voice of hysteria: You don't know for sure. There may be a logical explanation to why Corbin was out. Rainey even said so in the car on the way home.

This reasoning rings hollow and cold. Just like my insides as I begin my long hobble to the porch.

The evening air smells of fireplace smoke and a mélange of dinners cooking. Homey smells that make me sad.

The living room lights shine through the plantation shutters; the porch and the ambient yard lighting glow. For all intents and purposes one would think the stage was set for a warm welcome home.

I stand in front of the door for a minute, gathering

myself, getting into character so I don't go in and break down, blowing everything.

Yesterday, when I met with Hal Washington, private investigator, we decided it would be best for me to pretend everything was normal for the time being.

Easy for him to say.

It will be the performance of a lifetime, despite how many times I mentally rehearsed my homecoming yesterday while I lay on Alex's couch with my iced, bandaged foot propped on pillows. All I have to do is open the door, walk in, hug Caitlin, kiss Corbin—

Pricks of fury flow up and down my spine. Kissing him after he's been kissing God knows who?

I don't want him to touch me. But if I don't act normal Corbin will be suspicious and unless he's a real idiot, he'll most likely follow the straight and narrow, thereby prolonging Hal's task of catching him in the act.

If I act normal, Corbin will carry on and…well, the rest will soon be history.

I ease my key into the lock. Jack barks as I let myself in. The dog jumps up to greet me, knocking me off balance. I brace myself on the door frame.

The television is blaring in the other room. One of Caitlin's PBS shows.

What would I normally do? Call out *Hello, I'm home*.

I can't find my voice, so I leave my suitcase in the foyer and walk into the living room. Caitlin's alone, sprawled on her stomach on the floor watching TV in her play clothes. Corbin hasn't bathed her or bothered to get her into her jammies, which takes my apprehension down a couple of pegs to simmering anger.

The house smells vaguely of the popcorn my daughter's eating and unwashed dog—Jack didn't get his bath this weekend, either. Of course there's no dinner waiting. I don't know why it would even enter my mind that Corbin might have thought ahead and ordered takeout or even pizza.

In the past, I would have fallen back on *well, at least he left the porch light on*. But not this time. Anger ripples along my spine. My humoring benefit-of-the-doubt days are over.

Caitlin, on the other hand, lying there so small and innocent does not deserve the brunt of my anger toward her father.

I sneak up behind her and whisper, "Boo!" and tickle her. Delighted screams fill the air. She wriggles out of my grasp and throws her arms around my neck.

"Mommy! You're home. I missed you so much."

I feel almost whole again holding her, except for that constant reminder that this is no longer a home, not a happy one, anyway. A pang courses through me over how I'm going to explain to my daughter why her daddy can't live with us anymore.

But I'm not going to think about it until Hal Washington presents proof positive.

I ease myself down beside Caitlin, favoring my sore ankle, wondering what she'll say about the alarm going off in the middle of the night. "Did you and Daddy have a good weekend?"

She's kneeling in front of me and has one arm draped over my shoulder. She shrugs, picks up a strand of my hair and twirls it around her finger. She nods and her eyes shine. "We took Jack to the dog park today. It was so much fun."

She falls into my lap, still playing with my hair.

I'm so tempted to ask her if anything out of the ordinary happened—*Babysitters? Burglar alarms?* "I'm glad you had a good time."

She hugs me again and whispers, "Did you bring my nail polish like you promised?"

Oh— In the midst of all the craziness, I didn't get back to the salon to get her pink polish. But I have a bottle of fuchsia in my bathroom I'll give her. Not really appropriate for a little girl—not really appropriate for me, either. I got it for my toenails, wore it once, but the color was too bright. Caitlin can have fun with it. She'll love the color and never know that it came from my cosmetics bag rather than the Palm Beach salon.

"I do have some nail polish for you."

She springs to her feet and jumps up and down. "Can I have it now? Will you paint my nails tonight so I can wear it to school tomorrow?"

I nod. "First, I have to unpack and say hello to Daddy. Where is he?" Vague twinges of anxiety twitter in my stomach, but I have to face him sooner or later.

"He's up in his office talking on the phone."

Caution flares go off in my mind. Caitlin settles back on the floor to watch the rest of her program.

"Who's he talking to?"

She shrugs. A dancing hippopotamus on the big screen has snared her attention. I get to my feet feeling less graceful than the animated character.

"So, did I miss anything fun while I was gone?" *Careful, you're pushing it.*

She stares at the TV. "Nope. It was really boring without you."

Hmm. Well, how about that? I suppose she could have slept through the alarm. Sometimes I think a train could come through the house and it wouldn't wake her up. But… Well, it's okay. In fact, it's best she doesn't know anything's wrong right now. Corbin obviously got home before Caitlin woke up. Jenny probably paged him when the alarm went off.

Whatever.

I hobble into the foyer to get my suitcase.

It's difficult to navigate the stairs with my bag and my bum ankle, but I manage. Yesterday, I considered not even unpacking when I got home. One of the dozens of scenarios I hatched was to come in and grab Caitlin and leave.

Looking down the dark hall from the top step, I see light shining out from under Corbin's closed office door. I'm tempted to slip into Caitlin's room, pack a bag, grab her blankie and a few special toys and leave.

No note.

No hint about where we've gone.

Just disappear for a night or two. A rush of satisfaction washes over me at the horror and shock he'll feel when he goes downstairs to find the front door unlocked and his daughter gone. That'll teach him.

I shudder.

No, it probably won't. I'm sure in his mind he's found some way to compartmentalize both lives he's leading. I'm sure guilt over one would never cross his chauvinistic mind should he think we'd gone missing.

Besides, it would be dirty pool. Even as mad as I am at him, I can't be that mean. And Alex's words flood to the forefront of my mind.

"Whatever happens, never, ever leave your home or he can turn it around on you and say that *you* abandoned him."

That's one of the perks of having a best friend who's a divorce attorney, even though she can't handle my divorce should it come to that. She said since she knows both of us, ethics prevent her from representing either of us.

"But you can bet I'll set you up with the person I'd have represent me."

Corbin's laughter carries through the closed door. I pause outside and press my ear against the cold wood. He's talking in such a low voice I can't hear what he's saying, but I can tell by the sexy, flirty intonations and patterns of speech he's talking to a woman.

My blood boils. Before I think through the consequences, I throw open the door and stand there with my hands on my hips as if I've caught him red-handed.

He swirls around in his chair, puts his hand over the mouthpiece of his cell phone and says, "For God's sake, Kate, you scared me to death." He glares at me as if he's waiting for me to leave so he can finish his call, but I stand there until he finally says, "Hey listen, good talking to you, but I have to run. Kate just got home. Bye."

He hangs up and tosses the cell phone on his desk. I'm dying to ask why he's talking on the cell rather than the regular phone, but I know why. He's crafty. He's obviously thought this through so he won't get caught.

Well, little does he know.

It takes every ounce of strength I possess, but I hold my tongue. Corbin's a smooth talker. No doubt he'd be able to explain away everything. But I'm beyond wanting whitewashed explanations.

I'll let Hal Washington provide the proof—one way or the other.

"You're home. I didn't hear you come in."

Of course you didn't. How could you over all the laughing and cooing?

"Jack made a pretty loud racket. You didn't hear him?"

"No." He gives me a peck on the lips and brushes past me. He goes into the bedroom.

"Did you have a good time?"

I look at his cell phone sitting in the middle of the desk.

"Yes. Great time."

There'll be a log of placed and received calls inside his cell. If I can get a hold of it for even five minutes, I can get the number and give it to Hal...or call it myself. Yes, from his cell phone in case she has caller ID. Then I'll hang up.

"What did you do to your ankle?" Corbin brushes past me back into the office. He walks to the desk, picks up the phone and sticks it in his pocket.

Shit.

"I fell off my four-inch heels and twisted it."

Tonight. Tonight when he's sleeping I'll get it and check. That'll be the best time to call her...in the middle of the night when she thinks the rest of his family is sleeping, and he's calling for a little midnight phone sex.

She'd be just the type who would do that. I've never been able to talk dirty. I've never found anything sexy or appealing in it. A few months ago when we made love he started saying *Oh, yeah, fuck me, baby* and it pulled me totally out of the moment. Zap. Just like that. He'd *never* said anything like that in the middle of sex. I guess he felt me tense up. *Come on, Kate, what's wrong with you? It's all in fun. Come on, say it—fuck me, baby.*

God damn bastard. Now I know why.

He walks up to me and grabs me by the hips and pulls me into him. "Why did you fall? Were you out doing a little dirty dancing? I know what you girls do when you get away from the family."

He grinds his hips into me. I stumble backward and wince at the pain of putting full weight on my foot. "What are you talking about? We didn't go dancing. We don't *do* anything different when we're away than we'd do when we're at home."

Other than focusing on ourselves rather than being at your beck and call. But that's beside the point.

"Why, Corbin? Were you doing a little dirty dancing yourself this weekend? I read that when people feel guilty, they project their own transgressions onto their spouses."

His face stays blank. His gaze doesn't waver.

"Sure. Right. Like I could do anything this weekend while I had babysitting duty. Did you have your ankle checked to make sure it's not broken?"

"No, I didn't want to go to the emergency room or a walk-in clinic. I'm sure it's fine."

"All right. Then what are we doing for dinner? I'm starved."

I lay awake for hours after Corbin goes to sleep. Around two-thirty I get up and find the pants he was wearing earlier and check the pockets.

No cell phone.

I find it in his desk drawer. After locking the office door, I sit in his chair. The smooth cool leather creaks underneath me. I hold the phone under the soft glow of the desk lamp and scroll to the call log. My heart beats so furiously it hurts.

I wonder what her name is.

This is new territory for me. I've never felt the need to snoop and spy on my husband. I'm just not built that way. Not to mention, I've never had reason to dig for dirt.

This is different. Thinking about it shatters me. A tight knot of fear and dread intertwines in my stomach as I bring up the log of dialed calls.

It's empty?

Maybe she called him.

The received call register is empty, too.

I grit my teeth.

Corbin erased them.

It's like a scene from a movie.

I'm meeting Hal Washington, the private investigator, at nine-thirty on the park bench by the pagoda at Lake Eola in downtown Orlando.

After ten days on the job, he says he has *a little somethin'* for me. He won't go into detail on the phone. Just asks me to meet him in this very public but easy to escape place for the *handoff*.

He doesn't say it that way, of course, but why else would he ask me to meet him by the lake in the midst of all the joggers, businesspeople and mothers with toddlers feeding the swans and ducks?

I've seen how it works in the cheesy movies. He'll give me the envelope. I'll review the evidence—I hope I don't fall apart—I wonder if he'll hand me a handkerchief? Then he'll give necessary explanations and make his getaway, leaving me alone with my sorrow.

Just like in the movies.

Imagine if they met at a coffee shop—the P.I. would have to sit and finish his bagel while the client blubbered in her *grande* skinny latte.

Not fun. Hal's obviously done this a time or two.

I get to the bench about fifteen minutes early and sit down. Icy fear twists around my heart, and I can't feel my feet. It has nothing to do with my freshly healed sprain.

Corbin insisted I go into his office for X-rays just to make sure it wasn't broken. Then he gave me crutches and made sure I did what I needed to do to mend it.

He's a good doctor. The jerk. How can he be such a bastard and then turn around and do something like this that makes me want to forget all that's happened and retreat into the safe shell of our twenty-year marriage?

Too much has happened for me to forget now. If I think about sliding back into the way things used to be, all I have to do is anticipate the *little somethin'* Hal has in store for me.

I've been a wreck since he called me at eight-thirty this morning. He wouldn't have asked me to come if there was no news.

No news translates to good news.

A *little somethin'* means he's found something. In a matter of minutes the curtains will lift, and I will learn the naked truth.

Dear God,

I've never been a religious woman, but please make a miracle that turns this around. Please… keep my family together. If Hal brings evidence that Corbin's having an affair, my marriage is over.

I really wanted to believe in till death do us part.

A young couple strolls by, arms entwined. They're talking and laughing and making plans. I want to tell them to enjoy the fresh blush of love because it's not going to last. But a strong, cool gust of February wind blows away my words, and Hal slides in next to me on the bench.

CHAPTER 6

I always thought P.I.s gave their clients black-and-white photos. You know, delivering the evidence in black and white.

The pictures Hal Washington gave me were in vivid, living color and left very little to the imagination. If what they say about a picture being worth a thousand words is true, then there was nothing more to say after viewing these goodies of Corbin and a buxom blonde who Hal says is named Melody Wentworth. She's nineteen years old. Student by day, Orlando Magic dancer by night.

On the nights when she's not in bed with my husband.

It's all here—photos of Corbin and Melody Wentworth kissing in his car; holding hands outside the TD Waterhouse Centre where the basketball team plays; out on the town at dinner and nightclubs; pictures showing my Corbin's hands and mouth and body all over this woman who is young enough to be his daughter.

Corbin—or at least this man in the photos who looks like Corbin—is shameless. Did he not care that someone we know might see him? That word might get back to me that he is brazenly gallivanting around town with this bimbo?

Just as I predict, after Hal Washington, private investigator, drops the bomb in the neat little nine-by-thirteen manila envelope, he gives me the lowdown and excuses himself. I'm left to sit on the park bench in front of the red pagoda by Lake Eola and sift through the remnants of my life.

I don't cry. The numbness, formerly contained in my lower limbs, has now spread throughout my entire body. I sit there thumbing through the fifteen or so eight-by-ten glossy prints while the edges of my consciousness turn red and misty.

Oh wait, no—it's not *Misty*. It's Melody. Why does the other woman always have a name like *Melody*?

Melody. Say it—Mel-o-dy. The name rolls right off the tongue. Just like Melody rolled right into my husband's bed? Or should I say he rolled into her bed. I'd better not find out Mel-o-dy Wentworth has been anywhere close to my bed or—let's just say, the more I learn about this whole seamy affair, the more I can see how Lorena Bobbitt was perfectly justified.

I have Corbin's Jag today, his baby. The Lexus was making a noise, so he drove it to work to see if he could figure out the problem. If need be, he was going to have one of his assistants take it to the mechanic.

When I get in the car, I stare at the passenger seat. *She's* been in this car. Pictures don't lie. I want to take a knife to the fine leather upholstery and cut out the place where she sat.

Maybe I'll do that when I get home. Rip it to shreds and tape Melody's photo to the ruins with a note that says,

I found out what my lying bastard of a husband has been doing all those nights he said he was at the hospital.

I'll bet she wrote the letter. Only thing I *can't* figure out is if she's stupid for doing something so brazen or exceptionally conniving.

I ponder that conundrum for a while as I drive around, not really cognizant of where I'm going.

I say Melody's name aloud like a catty woman's mantra. When I say it, my upper lip curls back reflexively and my head does this side-to-side bob with each syllable. I can't help it.

"Mel-o-dy."

"Mel-o-dy."

I pound the steering wheel. Oh, how could Corbin be so unoriginal? So pathetically clichéd? Mel-o-dy Wentworth, the typical midlife crisis package: the same age as our oldest son; bleached blond hair; a cheerleader or dancer or whatever you call the bimbos who dance around center court wearing next to nothing— can you get any cheesier than that? She's packing the "nice set of D cups" that Dave Sanders is always trying to get me to submit to—

Oh my God. Dave knew. He knew all along and that's why he's been leering at me—well, he's been leering at me since day one, but Mac McCracken probably knows, too, and God knows who else.

Everyone but the wife.

I must look pretty pitiful blindly hanging in the balance of Corbin's dismal midlife crisis, with Mel-o-dy and her big boobs standing right there between us.

I'll bet everyone's been whispering *Kate has to know. She's blind if she doesn't.*

The Jag drives itself to the TD Waterhouse Centre. I stop in the street between the parking garage and the box office of the huge building. This is where Corbin enters for the games. He told me how cool it was to go behind the scenes.

Melody probably uses the same doors.

I don't know why I'm here, what I'm looking for. I pull out the photo of them outside the building and wonder exactly where it was taken. Given the nondescript background, I can't really tell.

So, instead, I sit and wonder whether he met her before or after he took the job as the Magic's team physician. And why, out of the smorgasbord of Magic dancers, did he choose her? According to photos she's cute, but not gorgeous. She has a perfect nineteen-year-old body—well, that'll go with age. She wears way too much makeup—probably justifies it because she wants to look good on camera during the televised games. Well, if she wants to look good, she needs to do something about that hair—frizzy overprocessed hair. She's obviously what we used to call a suicide blonde—died by her own hands. If she's not, her hairdresser deserves to be shot.

I pull out the ensemble publicity photo of the entire Hoosier dance team. Hal was good enough to include it in my goody bag. What was it about Mel-o-dy Went-worth that caught my Corbin's eye?

A sharp rap on the driver's side window makes me jump. I hit the photo on the steering wheel and it bends in half as I try to shove it out of sight from the security guard who's peering in at me.

I roll down the window.

"Everything all right, ma'am?"

No it's not. I'm sitting here contemplating a double homicide.

"Yes."

"This is a no-parking zone. I'm going to have to ask you to move your car."

I roll up the window without answering him and drive to Orange Avenue, the main street that runs through the downtown district. I pass the nightclub, Swingers, where Hal Washington said he shot one of the photos of Corbin and Mel-o-dy.

Swingers?

Oh, this is getting worse by the minute.

The traffic is too heavy to stop in front of the club, but I don't want to. I've seen enough.

Orange Avenue is a one-way street, and I follow it until I come to Anderson and go left.

"What am I going to do?" I drum my fingers on the steering wheel and pick up my cell phone to call my mother to ask her to take Caitlin for the evening. But I hang up before she answers. She'll think Corbin and I have a date or a function or some other happy reason to need alone time together. I don't have it in me to pretend. I also don't have it in me to lay the facts on the table. Not yet. My mother and father come from a long line of happily marrieds. They pride themselves on the fact that there's never been a divorce in the family.

It's going to kill them for their daughter to be the one to break the record.

My numb anger veers sharply into despondency as I turn left onto Bumby Avenue and stop for another red light.

I lay my forehead on the steering wheel and bawl.

"Damn him for doing this to me—to us. After all these years to throw it all away for a cheap dancer who's less than half his age." I lift my head up. "Good God, she's barely above the age of consent."

My temper flares again, and I'm breathless with rage.

A white convertible BMW pulls in behind me. A rap song blares so loudly from the open car I can hear it through my windows even though they're rolled up tight. The bass thumps through me like a hand keeping time on my breastbone.

I glance in the rearview mirror and catch a glimpse of my tearstained face as I watch the young blonde in the car behind me shimmy and sing along with the song. She's exactly the Mel-o-dy type. Young, tan, and pretty; not a care in the world. I'll bet Mel-o-dy drives a car like tha—

The blonde beeps her horn in time to the music. I realize the light's green, but before I can pull away she lays on the horn for a full five seconds. As I accelerate, she tailgates me, singing and dancing as the wind blows through her sun-streaked hair.

No one else is around. It's just the two of us on the straightaway. It's unbelievable how rude she's being. Damn it, why doesn't she just pass me? I tap my brakes, then speed up until the speedometer registers forty miles per hour. Still riding my bumper, she honks and gives me the middle finger.

And I don't know why I do it—but I gun the Jag then slam on the brakes.

"If my client says she stopped fast to avoid hitting a squirrel then that's what happened." Alex is talking to the police officer on my behalf. I called her instead of Corbin because I wasn't ready to face him.

I'm sitting on the curb, holding a tissue to my bloody nose—compliments of the air bag—while the paramedics check me to make sure I'm as okay as I claim I am. Thank goodness my nose isn't broken. Just a little mashed.

Corbin will freak when he sees the back end of his precious Jag, crushed like the tin cans he and his frat boy friends used to smash against their foreheads.

"That girl hit her from behind," says Alex. "There are no other witnesses. It's cut and dried."

I glance at the BMW. Its front end is compacted like an accordion. Guilt assails me. It was a stupid, *stupid* stunt. I was upset and I shouldn't have been driving. What if I had killed somebody?

Two paramedics are tending to BMW Girl.

"I'm not disputing she hit her from behind, ma'am," says the officer. He's probably about thirty-five. At that age, I wonder whose side he'll be more sympathetic to. The young thing or me? "What I'm asking is why she was traveling forty miles per hour in a twenty-five-mile-per-hour zone?"

I'm amazed that his demeanor is as calm as it is with Alex's rabid Perry Mason routine.

A paramedic packs my right nostril with cottony-gauzy stuffing. I wave away his suggestion to go to the hospital to be checked. This is the first I've heard of the squirrel who narrowly escaped with his life. I figure I'd better listen to what Alex is saying so our stories match.

"Look, Officer—" Alex glances at his name tag, gestures to it "—Adler, is it?" He nods. "Okay, look Officer Adler, was someone taking radar?"

I cringe, wishing Alex would soften her approach. But her style is more mad dog than lapdog. Although I really wish she wouldn't lie on my behalf.

"No, but we measured the skid marks."

"Can you prove they're from my client's car? Maybe the BMW was traveling too fast and had to skid to a stop before she *rear-ended* my client?"

Alex doesn't know about the photos yet. Speaking of— I stand and wobble, blink at the spots dancing before my eyes. I have to get the photos out of the car before the tow truck arrives.

The paramedic appears at my side, puts a hand to my elbow. "Lady, are you sure you don't want to go to the emergency room? I think you're suffering a little shock.

Sometimes you think you're fine, but later on it sneaks up on you. Hits you like a club."

Oh, how ironically lifelike that is. He's a cute boy. Looks as though he's in his early twenties—Melody Wentworth's age. He wouldn't have any idea of the blows life can deal. Hard enough to knock you flat.

"No, thank you. I'm fine."

"Okay." He shrugs and joins the others tending to BMW girl. She's sitting on the curb across the street bawling. Blubbering about how her boyfriend's going to kill her.

Boyfriend's car. Did I have that one pegged or what?

"It wasn't my fault." She wails and points at me. "The bitch hit the brakes on purpose. I know she did."

Shudders rack my body. I look away. I shouldn't have done what I did. *I shouldn't have done it.* And I'm not so sure I can let Alex keep up this phantom squirrel charade to get me off the hook. But as remorse wraps me in a tight cocoon, I realize I don't even know my left from my right. At least I have enough sense to keep my mouth shut until I'm thinking straight.

I stumble to the Jag's passenger side, and pull at the door. It sticks a little. I notice it's bent from the impact.

My knees nearly buckle. I grab the door frame until I'm steady.

I want to blame Corbin, but even in my state of nervous shock, I know I'm the one who must take responsibility for my actions.

Just as my husband will.

I reach in and grab the envelope off the floorboard, count the photos to make sure they're all there.

Out of my peripheral vision, I see a gray car slow to a stop beside me. A Cadillac. The tinted window slides down.

"Kate, hon? Is that you?"

Peg Sander's anxious face peers at me.

Oh great. Just what I need.

"What's happened?"

"I had a little accident, Peg. But I'm okay. Really, I am."

"Is Corbin here? That's his car."

I shake my head.

Peg's mouth forms a little O.

"Does he know?"

I grit my teeth and clutch the envelope to my chest.

The police wave Peg on before I have a chance to answer. I'm relieved when she complies and pulls away.

Alex walks up. "Who was that?"

"Peg Sanders, Corbin's partner's wife. The last person on earth I want to see right now. Well, maybe not the *last* person, but she's in the top five."

I glance around to see if anyone else is within earshot. "Why did you say I hit a squirrel?"

Alex gets these big deer-in-headlight eyes. "What? Didn't you? What other reason would you have for slamming on your brakes *with no warning?*"

This translates into, "I've gone out on a limb for you, Kate. Be a team player."

"Alex, it's a long ugly story. I'm just glad you weren't in court this morning."

She squeezes my shoulder. "If you had to have a wreck, your timing was certainly good. I'm glad I could be here for you, honey."

My cell phone rings from somewhere in the bowels of the car, but I don't have the energy to crawl under the air bag and dig it out.

Alex narrows her eyes. "This wouldn't have anything to do with Hal Washington, would it?"

Bile rises in the back of my throat and makes my eyes water. I can't speak because if I do I know I'll break down into a sobbing heap to rival BMW Girl's fit.

I thrust the envelope at her. She closes her eyes for

a minute before she accepts it, holding it as if it's infected with a communicable disease.

"Honey, I am so, so sorry."

I shrug, my composure slipping.

She pulls out the photos, shuffles through them, muttering things like, "Oh, pa-lease… Uggggggggh, give me a break… You must be kidding…so typical."

She shoves them back in the envelope and crosses her arms over them as if she's trying to render them invisible.

"If this is what he wants, he doesn't deserve you."

My mind is full of cobwebs. All I can do is stare at my sensible black Liz Claiborne pumps and wonder where I took the wrong turn to arrive at this sorry juncture in life?

"As far as I'm concerned, he's *never* deserved you," Alex says.

This makes me look up. Alex is jaded when it comes to men and marriage. She's a no-nonsense career woman who's never been married and is the first to admit the garbage she's witnessed in divorce court, coupled with her mother's promiscuous lifestyle, has permanently tainted her opinion of marriage. But in this case, she's right.

"He can be such a jackass sometimes, can't he?" I say.

"Sometimes? Oh my God. I don't know how you put up with him all these years. What are you going to do now?"

All these years. It hits me like a cold glass of water in the face. I inhale sharply. Tears sting my eyes and the inside of my bruised nostrils. "Who's asking that question—Alex, the divorce attorney or Alex, my friend?"

"You know I can't represent your divorce, as much as I'd like to take the son of a bitch for every cent he's worth. Right now, I'm the friend who'll shut up and listen. Okay?"

A slow, steady stream of traffic rolls by. People are rubbernecking to get a good look at the two totaled luxury cars.

"I don't know, Alex," is all I can manage. Everything I'd say if I poured my heart out is stuck in the cobwebs in my mind—things like how I drove around aimlessly all morning wailing like an injured animal; how I knew Corbin had checked out of this marriage a long time ago, but I didn't have the guts to face facts; that I'm scared and feel small and completely unlovable; and that there's a very real part of me that can't bear the thought of letting a lawyer pour verbal alcohol on my open wounds because given the chance right now, I might just turn the other cheek and pretend as though I'd never heard the name Melody Wentworth because I want my family. I want my old life. I want everything to be the way it used to be.

I try to speak, but I choke on a sob and the tears turn on like a broken water main.

I can't even stop crying when I hear footsteps behind us. It's Adler approaching. Beyond him, I see BMW Girl talking on her cell phone—ranting, raving, swearing, gesturing.

"Mrs. Hennessey, are you okay? Is she okay?" he says to Alex.

Alex shrugs. "It's her husband's car. He's going to be pissed."

Hearing this helps. Yes, he will. He'll be fit to be tied. The thought gives me some satisfaction. I swipe at my tears. Officer Adler gets some tissue from the medics.

"Thank you," I say.

"If you're up to it, I just need to ask you a couple of questions."

Alex steps between us, still holding that damned envelope. I don't think I'll ever be able to look at a manila envelope again without feeling sick.

"Kate, you don't have to answer any questions. Let me do the talking."

The officer sighs, talks to me. "Ma'am, you're not under arrest or in trouble. I just need your side of the story."

He sounds a little weary, as if Alex has pushed the bounds of his good nature to the limits.

I give him a rueful smile. He grins back.

"Just tell me in your own words what happened."

I take a deep breath and whisper a silent prayer that begs for forgiveness. "Well, there was this squirrel—"

A Lexus screeches to a halt beside us.

Corbin jumps out, blocking traffic, just as BMW girl trots up to Adler yelling, "You want to know what happened? I'll tell you—the bitch slammed on her brakes on purpose—that's what happened. I know she did it on purpose, and I'm going to sue her."

Corbin puts his hands on his hips.

"Kate? What the hell happened?"

CHAPTER 7

Strange what comes to mind in the midst of a crisis. Armed with the truth and faced with confronting Corbin, I'm not contemplating all the ways I'd torture him. I'm more preoccupied with important things like how in classical mythology the Greek goddess Hera was forced to defend her home and marriage against the infidelities of her husband, Zeus, and his attempts to humiliate her.

At face value it makes sense that I'd draw this parallel—a classic case of misery loves company; even the greatest goddess of them all couldn't keep her man from straying. But as Corbin drives me home, the envelope of pictures on my lap under my purse, I think on a deeper level, self-preservation kicks in and subconsciously I'm centering myself—summoning my inner goddess before marching into the battle of my life.

The moment of truth happens when we get home.

It took great restraint not to throw the photos in Corbin's face and kick him to the curb as we stood glaring at each other in the middle of the intersection. If I tore into him there, I'd have had to be civilized about it.

That was enough incentive to wait until we're home.

Alex couldn't believe I was up for letting him drive me home.

There's no other choice, I told her. *If he doesn't drive me home he'll go back to the office and it will have to wait until tonight. I need to take care of this before Caitlin comes home.*

Take care of this... It sounds like an embarrassing medical problem I've put off, hoping it would go away, or a traffic ticket I'd neglected to pay.

"Come inside for a minute," I say when we pull in the driveway. "I need to talk to you."

Corbin sighs, pushes his Armani sunglasses up on his nose.

"I've wasted an entire morning. I need to get back to the office."

"This can't wait."

I get out of the car and slam the door.

He kills the engine. I unlock the front door.

Jack jumps up and greets me as I step into the foyer. It's as if I'm seeing everything through a fish-eye lens;

same house, same dog—same foyer with its polished, hardwood floor and pricey Persian rug, same dark yellow envelope I've clutched since nine-thirty this morning, but it's all coming at me like the distorted images in a 3-D movie; accompanied by the disconcerting sound track of a barking dog, pounding heart and Corbin closing the front door behind me.

The goddess Hera represents the power of women to stand for what they know is right. She is a symbol of the women's struggle in a predominantly patriarchal society.

Because of this, she was sometimes seen as jealous, petty and spiteful.

A first-class bitch. I hand Corbin the photos and walk away.

"What's this?"

I don't answer him. I don't even look back. I've seen enough. For this, I believe the goddess Hera is smiling down on me, comforting me with the sweep of a gentle hand. *You are not undesirable, Kate. I, the mother of all goddesses, suffered similar indignity. You're in good company. You will be all right.*

I wish I had it in me to believe her instead of feeling big and frumpy and awkward and old as I ascend the staircase. But I'm not quite *that* in touch with my inner goddess.

"Shit," is all Corbin says. The word follows me upstairs, lingers with me on the landing. I clutch the banister and glance around the dim hallway, bewildered and displaced.

Caitlin's room is the first door on the right, next to Corbin's office, across the hall from our bedroom, down the hall from the guest room. If everything is in its place, why do I feel like a stranger standing in someone else's home?

I grasp the doorjamb and search for something familiar to fill me up before any more of me leaks away, and I become so flimsy that I float up and out into the stratosphere, eventually to be sucked into the black hole of the universe.

If that happens, who will care for Caitlin? She needs me. Because if not for me, who will teach her about the goddess Hera, and that you don't have to put up with the humiliation of cheating husbands.

Long, skinny rectangles of sunlight filter through the Plantation shutter slats and spill onto the floor. It makes me think of the lasagna noodles I cooked before I left for Palm Beach.

Does Melody Wentworth know how to cook lasagna? If not, she'd better learn because Corbin loves his lasagna. Or at least I thought he did. I guess I never really knew him very well.

"Kate?" Corbin's at the bottom of the stairs. "Can we talk about this?"

No. I don't want to talk to you. Can't you just go away? Just fade away and leave me alone so I can pretend like you died some tragic, heroic death. When people say, "Kate, we're so sorry." I can nod and mutter rueful sentiments like a good widow. Because isn't that what's happened? Hasn't our marriage just died?

The words won't budge. They're lodged between my heart and my throat. I don't know what to do, where to go. I hear his footfalls as he jogs up the steps.

Before he gets to the top, I lock myself in the bedroom. When he pounds on the door, and begs me to let him in, to talk about this because he *loves me*, I retreat into the bathroom and run water in the sink, turn on the bathtub faucet and the shower. I do this not only to cover his pleas, but also to drown the voice inside urging me to open the door and give him a chance to explain it all away. So we can put it behind us and be a family.

Well, I am not Mrs. Robinson and I refuse to *hide it in the pantry with my cupcakes*. A little secret just the Hennesseys will share…

I don't think I can hurt any worse than I do at that moment. But I'm wrong. I hurt much, much more in the ensuing hush when Corbin stops knocking and the house falls silent.

I venture out of the bathroom about an hour later because I have to get Caitlin from school. I peer out the foyer window to make sure he's really gone and not silently lurking in the living room or kitchen to trick me into discussing the photos.

The driveway's empty—good. No! Not good! That *bastard!* I can't believe the idiot took the car. I know he had to go back to the office or to confer with Melody Wentworth or wherever he might be inclined to go to do whatever it is he does when we're apart, but I can't believe the bastard wouldn't even think about his daughter.

Caitlin goes to a private school on the other side of town. She doesn't ride a bus. It's not as if I can walk to get her.

I let the sheer drape fall back into place. Jack is lying on the floor with his head resting on his paws. He seems to have a worry crease between his bug-brown eyes. He sighs only the way dogs can sigh and looks up at me with an apologetic expression that suggests he feels my pain.

I reach down to pet him contemplating whether I should call a cab to take me to pick up Caitlin from school or impose on the mother of one of her friends to bring her home. I don't carpool with anyone, and I've never been comfortable asking anyone to fetch my child. One of the drawbacks to private school is that her classmates are scattered all over town. It would be a big inconvenience to ask them to go out of their way to bring her home. I'm mulling over asking Rainey to take me—I need to tell her what's happened anyway—when a slow-dawning horror reaches out and wraps its bony fingers around my spine.

What if Corbin— No… He wouldn't dare—

I run into the kitchen and dial the number for Caitlin's school. It takes an eternity for someone to answer. "Liberty School, this is Marge. How may I help you?"

My mind races trying to come up with a plausible reason why I'd worry about Caitlin's father picking her up from school without airing my dirty laundry. I glance around the kitchen looking for a clue.

Forgotten lunch box? No, too late for that.

Missed medicine that he was dropping off? Maybe...

My gaze snares a note on the calendar.

"Hello?" says Marge. "Is anyone there?"

I sniff. "Yes, sorry. Hi, Marge. This is Kate Hennessey. I was calling because..." My stomach clenches, but I force out the words hoping the excuse doesn't sound as flimsy and bogus as it feels. "This is quite embarrassing, actually. I'm so disorganized lately.... I thought Caitlin had a dentist appointment today. As it turns out the appointment's next week. My husband was going to take her today. I tried to get in touch with him when I realized the mistake, but I haven't been able to connect with him. Please tell me he hasn't been there to pick her up yet."

"No, he hasn't, Mrs. Hennessey."

"Great. Thank you."

"You're welcome. May I help with anything else?"

"Yes, if he does come, don't release Caitlin to him—"

I cringe at how it sounds.

"Well...he is one of her legal guardians...."

"Oh, yes, right... What I mean is, please tell him the dentist appointment isn't today and that I'm on my way."

"Okay." Her tired voice implies that she thinks I'm a loon. I thank her and hang up as fast as I can.

I blow my nose and glance at the clock. Caitlin's still got an hour and a half of school left.

More than likely if Corbin didn't get her when he left, he won't bother—I sit down at the kitchen table and dial his office. Each ring feels like a heavy weight dropped inside my head. My stomach churns and plummets when Janet, his administrative assistant, answers with a perky, "Dr. Hennessey's office."

"Um, yes, hi, Janet. This is Kate Hennessey, is my…husband in?"

Blood pounds in my ears.

"Yes, Mrs. Hennessey, hi. How are you today?"

Oh, if you only knew… "I'm very well, and you?"

"Fine, thanks. If you'll hold for a minute I'll get him. He's with a patient."

"Oh no, don't bother him. It's not important."

"It's not a problem. In fact, he told me to put you right through if you called. Just a moment."

Put me right through? The song "Let It Be" drifts over the line, and satisfied with the knowledge Corbin is at his office, I hang up.

I decide not to call Rainey because I don't want to

uncork the dam I've so neatly constructed around my emotions. I need to be stable, normal when I pick up my daughter from school.

Caitlin will get a kick out of riding in a cab. She'll think it's fun. I'll turn it into an adventure. Maybe we'll have the driver take us all over town. Have him wait outside while we go to dinner. *Oh, just let the meter run.* I grab the Yellow Pages. I've hailed a taxi in Manhattan, but I've never had the need to call a cab in Orlando.

I flip to the C listings for cab— No, wait... I need the T section for taxicabs.

There's a bunch—Emerald Taxi Service... Orlando Executive Taxis... Yellow Cab Company... But it's the large display ad featuring a uniformed driver standing between black and white stretch limousines that catches my eye.

Alibi Luxury Cars.

Alibi? This is too good.

The ad says:

You don't need an excuse to travel in style. We'll be your Alibi. Chauffeured cars, vans and limousines available in the metro Orlando area within an hour's notice.

My heart aches at the thought of Corbin coming up with excuses to explain away the photographs. As if that was possible. I don't want his excuses or his alibis.

I imagine him looking me in the eye and saying, "Kate, that's not me. Granted, the guy looks like me, but you can see his ears are completely different than mine—"

Scratch the taxicab.

I'm going for the limo. If I'm going to teach my daughter to demand men treat her right, then I need to teach her to treat herself right first.

I order a traditional black limo first, but then change my mind and ask for the white stretch model because I think Caitlin will like a white car better.

"No white ones today, lady. Only black."

Oh.

"Well, I suppose black will do."

"'Kay, it's a hundred bucks an hour, tip not included, four-hour minimum. You down with that?"

Am I down with that? I picture a pockmark-faced punk with greasy hair and at least two-dozen heavy gold rope chains adorned with bling-encrusted license plates hanging around his skinny little neck. Bling—see, I'm not so out of it. In my mind, he's sitting with his legs stretched out on top of a desk, the same obnoxious rap tune BMW Girl was listening to blaring in the background—even though the phone line is perfectly quiet.

Not exactly the kind of reception I expected from an organization that deals in luxury cars—but then again with a name like *Alibi* what can one expect? I got my limo—and on such short notice, too.

"That's perfect."

I imagine Hera doing a little dance and saying, *You go, girl.*

After the order is placed, I run upstairs to freshen my makeup and change clothes—and carefully avoid looking in the direction of Corbin's office. Maybe I'll renovate it into a playroom for Caitlin once he gets his belongings out.

Back downstairs, I sit in the chair by the window to watch for the driver. I glance at my watch. Fifteen minutes until the driver is supposed to arrive. That's not so bad. It'll give me a chance to collect myself.

Exactly three minutes later, I'm antsy. I start replaying the meeting with Hal Washington in my mind; the accident; Corbin arriving and saying, "What the hell happened?"

I pace the length of the beige living room four times

before I grab my *Architectural Digest* off the coffee table and sit back down in my seat by the window to look at it.

The gorgeous colors and lavishly decorated homes featured in the issue make my beige room seem like a monochromatic padded cell.

I flip past a furniture ad to the section with the lushly decorated Moroccan living room I liked so much. It explodes off the page.

Wow. Now, that's nice.

The tangerine walls handwashed with sheer gold to give it a distressed look set the room ablaze; the ceiling is tented with beautiful tapestry boasting colors like rust, azure, grape, ruby and aquamarine. Inviting pillows are scattered on the floor, beckoning revelers to sink down into them.

I can almost smell the incense and the curry.

Instead of a sofa there's a raised platform covered in the same fabric that's on the ceiling; it's scattered with pillows and more pillows—large and small, in prints and solids of vivid jewel tones, with tassels and buttons and pieces of mirror that sparkle like diamonds.

The image takes me back to my more adventurous days of design school when I would have likely created something like this, when my ideas would have never been the boring, monochromatic shades of beige that I tried to pass off as understated and elegant.

Boring by any other name is still boring.

I glanced around the room mentally imposing the Moroccan room over the blank beige canvas.

"Corbin would hate it."

Hera says, *Corbin won't be living here much longer.*

The breath escapes my body, as if someone pulled the plug on a raft. The magazine slides from my lap as I bend over and rest my head in my hands and sob until the tears spill down my arms.

I remember when Corbin and I bought the beige-on-beige couch. We shopped for it together. Chose it together. Came home and made love on that beige-on-beige couch.

No, Corbin, Daniel could walk in any minute.

Come on, we'll hear him before he hears us.

He wanted me then. And at that moment you couldn't have convinced me distressed tangerine and gold-washed walls would've been more exciting than *our* beige-on-beige sofa.

But the kaleidoscope of my mind's eye shifts, and it's not me Corbin's making love to on our couch—it's Melody Wentworth. My eyes fly open and all I can see for a minute is the blurry imprint the heels of my hand left on my vision.

Then the dark streaks of mascara transferred by my tears to my hands and arms come into focus, and the beige-on-beige couch that is no longer *our* couch.

I get up and wipe the wet mascara streaks on the cushions.

"That's for lying to me."

Not quite satisfied by the dirty smudge, I grab the Baccarat decanter that holds Corbin's 1936 Château de Castex d'Armagnac cognac and upend it over the couch. The heavy crystal top smashes on the beige marble cocktail table. I move the bottle over the cushions so that each of the three sections gets a good soaking.

"That's for throwing away our family."

I choke on a sob and am tempted to get a match so I can watch the whole ugly thing burn, but that would be arson. I've already caused one impulsive accident today. I don't need another added to my conscience's rap sheet.

Instead, I grab the potted philodendron and layer the potting soil over the cognac and walk on it, grinding in the dirt with my foot.

"That's for sending the twenty years I've invested in this marriage down the shitter."

The knock on the door startles me. For a second I'm afraid it's Corbin catching me in the act. For a split second I feel like a naughty child.

Corbin wouldn't knock.

And to hell with his disapproval. I drop the crystal decanter on the coffee table—it shatters—and I wipe my nose on my sleeve.

As I glance out the window at the black stretch limo in the driveway, I make a mental note to tell Caitlin to stay out of the living room until I can vacuum.

I wouldn't want her to cut herself.

Hera says, *Madame, your chariot has arrived*.

I brush the dirt from my hands, wipe the lingering tears from my face, grab the *Architectural Digest* and my purse and set out to take Caitlin on the adventure of her life.

"Mommeeeeeeeeee? I don't want to ride in this big, ugly car. It looks like the ones they use to move dead people. Where's our car? I want our car."

Caitlin refuses to get in the limo, and we're holding up the car line. "Sweetie, Daddy has our car. This is a limousine. *Everyone* wants to ride in a limousine."

She crosses her arms over her navy-and-red-plaid

uniform jumper and dons one of Corbin's exasperated expressions.

"Not me! You're embarrassing me. Your face is dirty and this is a scary car, and I can't believe you brought it to my school."

Jocelyn Morgan, PTA president and career volunteer, is helping the staff load the students into cars. "Wow, Caitlin, you are a lucky girl to get to ride in a *limousine*. Is it your birthday?"

Sullen, Caitlin stares at her shoes and doesn't answer. I have the strangest sensation she knows what's happened. She never acts like this—so outwardly defiant.

But how can she know what's happened between Corbin and me? She's just a little girl, and she's been at school all day.

Jocelyn pokes her head in the car door and does a double take. "Kate? Are you okay? Have you been crying?"

I sink deeper into the cordovan colored leather seats and wave away her concern. "I'm fine. Just one of those days."

"I suppose so." Jocelyn brushes a wisp of short, jet-black hair out of her eyes and takes a good, long perusal of the inside of the car. "We don't get many limousines through the car line." She grits her teeth and shoots me a what-the-hell-am-I-going-to-do-to-top-this-for-my-daughter smile. "Is this a special occasion?"

I don't know. Is divorce a special occasion?

I shake my head. "Car's in the shop."

She quirks a brow. "Oh. I see. Caitlin, dear, get in now. Your *limousine* is holding up my car line."

CHAPTER 8

I finally discover that Caitlin didn't want to get in the limo because the car reminded her of the hearse they used to take Grandpa Hennessey's body to the grave last year.

I guess to a child all big black cars look alike. When it pulled up and they called her name to get in, she thought someone she loved had died. I'm sure it didn't help seeing my tearstained, dirty face when she looked inside. I had no idea I looked like such a mess.

I'm mortified. In hindsight, perhaps the black limousine wasn't appropriate after all.

But it doesn't take long for her to cheer up. We take a quick detour to Home Depot to buy paint for the living room. Next, we run through the McDonald's drive-through. We both order cheeseburger Happy Meal combos and strawberry shakes and have the driver take us to Millennia Mall while we eat and talk about her day.

After we shop ourselves to exhaustion, the limo picks us, and all our packages, up at the Nordstrom store entrance—just like I arranged. Despite the circumstance surrounding it, it's fun.

Caitlin crawls into my lap and lays her head on my shoulder. I survey the bags and boxes acquired during my *shopping therapy*. Nothing like it when the credit card you're using carries a very large limit and is billed to an unfaithful husband.

Hey, either I spend the money on my daughter and myself or he spends it on *her*.

So Caitlin got some new clothes and shoes; some fun and funky bedroom accessories from a shop called Dry Ice; a new duvet cover and curtains from Pottery Barn Kids. I bought a bouquet of exotic flowers from a cart in the center of the mall; a bottle of patchouli oil—Corbin hates patchouli oil; he thinks it smells like cat pee—and a diffuser to burn it in; new towels as big as twin sheets; new pajamas and cotton undies—no more pretty but sadistically uncomfortable lingerie for me, thank you—a four-pound gold ballotin of Godiva chocolate. I contemplated getting a pound for each year of our marriage, but I didn't want twenty-plus pounds to show up on the scale. One hundred and forty pieces of chocolate is plenty.

From now on, I shall take care of me.

I shall eat my Godiva while lounging on my new three-hundred-and-thirty-thread-count Kate Spade sheets with coordinating comforter set.

You should see my new comforter—a gorgeous motif of red and antique gold. Exquisite. It'll go perfectly with the Scarlett O'Hara paint.

Darn it! I was so fixated on tangerine and gold to go with the yards and yards of Moroccan tapestry I ordered via my cell phone and the handy number listed in the back of *Architectural Digest* magazine's product information section that I completely forgot about Scarlett.

Oh well, there's always tomorrow. If I don't have my car back, I'll call my *Alibi*.

Bloomingdale's said they'll deliver the new bed the day after tomorrow. So I'll have to make sure I'm home.

There's something to be said about spending a little more for quality. I really can tell the difference between the ten-thousand-dollar Shifman I purchased tonight and the old Stearns & Foster we've slept on for the past eight years.

No wonder my back's been aching.

I heard somewhere that the first step a divorced woman should take in her new life is to buy a new bed.

It symbolizes a fresh start. Shoos out the bad energy. You know, out with the old, in with the new.

The new bed is mine and mine alone.

No lingering essence of Melody Wentworth in my bedroom.

And I'm not even divorced yet. Let's call it being proactive. I'm tired of sitting around having things happen to me. From this day on, I am taking charge of my life.

I just wish someone could tell me an easy way to explain divorce and all it means to a young and innocent child. I smooth Caitlin's tangled curls off her forehead. Her eyes are closed. She's had a big day.

I tighten my arms around her. If I'm so *in charge*, how on earth am I going to make it through shipping her back and forth between two households and how am I going to explain that from now on she won't be able to spend holidays with both of her parents?

I can't imagine Christmas Eve—or any other special occasion—without her. Corbin probably can't, either, but he should have thought about that before he let his libido dictate his destiny.

I look out the window at the billboards lining Interstate Four advertising various local theme parks. The limo's wheels hum a hypnotic tune that lulls me into a surreal place—somewhere between hypercalm and quiet hysteria. My mind is racing, but my body's exhausted. I don't even have the energy to move. Maybe it's the way the car's gently swaying, as if an invisible hand is rocking our giant cradle.

If Caitlin and I could stay like this forever, Corbin could have the house. Caitlin and I will live in this limo and have the chauffeur drive us around and around. Because in here we are far removed from the rest of the world. In here, we need not concern ourselves with the day or the time or place; as far as we're concerned, out there there's only the Magic Kingdom and Sea World and Islands of Adventure. Happy places where it won't matter if it's Caitlin's weekend to be with me or her holiday to spend with Corbin…

Caitlin stirs.

"Mommy, when are we going home?" She rubs her eyes and lays her head back on my shoulder. My arms are still around her, but the tentacles of reality permeate my insulated little cocoon.

"Are you ready to go?"

She nods.

I glance at my watch. It's nine-thirty. Way past her

bedtime. It's not fair to keep her out late just because I don't want to go home and close this chapter of my life.

Hera says, *How can you be so sure it's over? You haven't even given him a chance to explain.*

Whose side are you on?

I'm disappointed that the mother of all goddesses would even give Corbin a voice. It's not going to change anything. She of all people should know that once the vow is broken it can never be mended.

She pipes up, *I suffered a great many times in the face of Zeus's infidelities. Love can heal a great many things. If you love him. Do you love him, Kate?*

Do I love him?

I can't answer that right now.

When the limousine pulls into the driveway, it's like a spaceship reentering the earth's atmosphere and splashing down in the tumultuous sea. A sleepy Caitlin and I step out of the warm car into the chilly night air.

Back to reality.

She staggers up the walk half asleep. I tip the driver $150 after he carries my paint and packages to the porch. I consider asking him to hide the booty around the side of the house, but by that time, he's already getting in his car, and Caitlin is already banging the door knocker.

What am I going to say to Corbin?

What is there to say? *Well, it's been fun. Have a nice life?*

I wonder what he thought when he got home and we weren't there—that I'd gone to my mother's house or Rainey's or Alex's? He probably thought we weren't coming home tonight.

I'm still standing in the driveway when the sleek, black automobile pulls away like a panther prowling the night. A sickening thought creeps into my mind. What if he's with *her?* What if he thought we weren't coming home and went to *her?*

The front door opens and my little girl flings her arms around her Daddy's legs. I'm flooded with a strange emotion I can't quite identify—part bittersweet relief that he is home and not with Melody; part dread at having to face him. He kneels and pulls her into his arms, buries his face in her hair, then looks out at me. I'm rooted to the ground. I can't make my feet move.

I know it's inevitable that we'll have to talk, but I don't want to face him in front of Caitlin. I don't want to go in and pretend everything is normal. I don't want to know if he's mad about the mess I made in the living room and all the things I bought at the mall.

I just don't want to deal with it right now.

Jack barks and Caitlin disappears inside after him.

Corbin stands in the doorway in a white polo shirt and jeans, and I hate him for how good he looks. I hate myself for the pang that pierces me at the memory of how his body feels and how his cocky good looks and sophisticated charm swept me off my feet.

I loved him. I really loved him and right now it hurts so damned much that I want to melt into a river of emotion and flow away.

I have no idea how long we've been standing there when he finally says, "Kate, please come inside." All I know is that I'm chilled to the bone; two cars have driven by and a neighbor we don't know ran by with his Great Dane.

By the grace of God, somehow my legs carry me up to the porch and into the house. Caitlin is lying on the kitchen floor playing with Jack.

Corbin carries in my packages and all he says is, "I'm glad you're home. I was worried."

Corbin is still awake after I put Caitlin to bed. He's sitting at the kitchen table with an open bottle of Opus

One Cabernet and two glasses. He's set out some Saga blue and Carr crackers on the marble cheese tray. To the right of the tray sits a dozen red roses and a black velvet jewelry box.

He stands when I enter the room. So formal, so polite. "Did you have dinner?"

I don't know what to say—Caitlin told him about how I picked her up from school in the limo and how we went through the McDonald's drive-through. I'm surprised he hasn't said anything about that or the paint and packages that are still in the foyer. For all his pretentious airs, more often than not he's a frugal fuddy-duddy. Not that there's anything wrong with frugality. Limousines and Baccarat crystal are so far removed from how I was raised.

Sometimes I don't even know how I got here—in this fancy house, driving my fancy car, living this hated country club life with my fancy doctor husband who cheats—"I'm not hungry, thanks."

He stares at his hands clasped in front of him, makes a jerky movement as he simultaneously grabs a goblet and pulls out a chair for me. "Then sit, have some wine. Please?"

"No thank you."

"Kate." He steps toward me.

I step back, turn to leave.

"Did Melody send the letter?" I ask without looking at him.

He sighs. "Yes."

That's all I need to know. I start to walk away.

"Kate, please…just tell me what you want me to do. I'll do anything to make it right."

He says the words to my back.

I shake my head *no*, moving it so fast and furiously from side to side that the blues and yellows of the kitchen spin and merge with the stainless steel appliances. The rooster on the oil painting we bought in Montmartre on our last trip to Paris does a maniacal dance. It reminds me of how the world spun when we rode the carousel near *Sacré-Coeur*.

I grab the doorjamb.

"I want you to go. I want you out of my life."

I close my eyes waiting for him to correct me. *I'll never be completely out of your life, Kate, because we'll be forever joined by our children.*

Our children.

The children we made when life was good.

Does Melody Wentworth want children?

I whirl around. "When did things change, Corbin? When did it all go bad? Tell me, because I can't remember."

He looks puzzled, as if I'm speaking Greek. I know he doesn't know when it all went wrong any better than I do.

I sigh and walk out of the room.

He follows me upstairs.

"We'll have to talk about this eventually. If you really want me to move out—and I would hope you'd think long and hard about that for Caitlin's sake—I'll have to find a place. I can't just pack a bag and go."

"Shhhhhhhh!" I point to Caitlin's room, walk over and shut the door.

It's on the tip of my tongue to tell him to go stay with his girlfriend, to teach him a lesson like when you give a child free rein over her own Halloween bag. Let him have so much Melody Wentworth he makes himself sick and barfs.

I walk into our bedroom and stand in front of our big, sad bed; I realize that though I don't want him here, I don't want him with *her* even more.

I grab his pillow and toss it to him.

"You can sleep in the guest room until you make new arrangements."

For once, Corbin, we're doing things on my terms.

I'm up to my elbows in paint when the doorbell rings. I don't answer it. I don't even climb down from my ladder, just keep painting and singing along with Simon and Garfunkel's "I am a Rock."

Nothing like a good song to help you express exactly what's on your mind. That's why I programmed Caitlin's boom box to play the song over and over. An endless loop of go-to-hell-I-am-better-without-you song. I wanted to broadcast it over Corbin's stereo so I could turn up the speakers as high as they'd go and blast the song in every room of the house like a feng shui space-cleaning ritual working in conjunction with the patchouli oil I'm burning in the diffuser. With all the buttons and knobs, I couldn't figure out how to program the stereo, so I settled for the old reliable.

That's all I want—something simple and reliable. Is that asking for too much?

I give the roller a generous coating of paint and cut a bright orange swath over the wall, singing about how if I'd never loved I never would have cried.

A hand touches my leg.

I scream and nearly fall off my ladder, dropping my roller in the process. Paint splatters all over the beige Berber carpet.

"Oh, I'm sorry." My mother bends and picks up the roller, hands it to me. "Quick, where's a rag so I can blot this? Oh, I can't believe I made you drop it. I'm just glad you didn't fall."

She grabs the old towel I've draped over the ladder and gets down on her hands and knees.

"Mom, don't worry about it. I'm going to pull it up anyway."

She stops blotting and looks up at me.

"Why aren't you answering your door? Didn't you hear me ring the bell?"

I stare at her, not quite sure what to say, wanting to say, I heard you ringing. *Don't you know when some-one doesn't answer the door it means they don't want company?*

But I don't say it. My mother is much too sweet to deserve such snide insolence.

Simon pronounces the final line of the song, sing-ing about a rock feeling no pain, and an island never crying. I want to say, *what he said. I didn't answer it be-*

cause I don't need anyone—except maybe my children—
Oh, okay, and you.

"Sorry. I'm in the middle of painting and I thought you were a Jehovah's Witness. We get so many of them around here I've quit answering the door when I'm busy."

The song starts over. I wipe my hands on my overalls, glance at the stained couch, feeling a little guilty. I climb down and turn off the boom box. When I look up, my mother is eyeing the wall, wearing a dubious expression.

"What do you think?"

"Pretty, but it's awfully bright, isn't it? But what matters is that you like it." She smiles, but it's not her normal gracious smile, and I sense something's wrong before she says, "Kate, I need to talk to you about your father."

"Is everything all right?"

She eyes the couch, the tricolored brown pattern the cognac, dirt and mascara created on the beige sofa. I can see she's choosing her words.

"Your father's blood count came back high. The doctor says the cancer's back. It's spread to his liver."

Her words roll over me. I can't speak, I can't move. All I can do is stand there gripping the ladder, hoping I didn't hear her right.

She laughs a morbid, nervous laugh. "The doctor says it could be three months, could be three years. But you know your father, he says he's going to live to one hundred just so he can make everyone else miserable. He's just got to be fine. Tell me he's going to be fine—"

Her hand flies to her mouth and she starts to sob.

"I'm so sorry." I walk over and pull her into a hug, and she cries. We stand there together; she, limp as a rag doll, I, stiff as a stone statue.

It's not because my heart isn't breaking all over again for the second time in twenty-four hours. In fact, I'm pretty sure it's ground to the consistency of powdered glass. So, fine—I don't have any sharp edges left.

Well, maybe I have one. The one I'm clinging to desperately right now, knowing that if I let go I'll slide down into the black hole of grief and never find my way out.

"I'll make us some tea," I whisper.

I forget about the four-pound box of Godiva, sitting well pillaged next to the roses and unopened jewelry case until I see it all sitting on the table like a shrine to our broken marriage when we walk into the kitchen.

Mom's teary gaze lingers over the items, and she

quirks a brow. "Those are awfully pretty roses." She sniffs. "Did I miss something?"

I hand her a tissue from the box on the shelf, shake my head, trying to concoct a plausible excuse for such extravagant gifts. But anything I say will make Corbin look good. So I don't say anything.

She blows her nose, sniffs again. "There's only two occasions a man gives jewelry and roses like that to his wife—when there's something to celebrate or something to be sorry for."

She tucks the tissue in her pocket, picks up the black velvet box and opens it. Her mouth flattens into a thin line; her eyes flicker to me.

"You don't turn forty for another few months. Your big twenty-year anniversary celebration has already passed. Do you have something you need to talk about?"

I feel myself slipping, the black hole closing around me. If I don't say anything I'll be okay. But she's standing there looking at me, expectant. I have to say *something*.

"Everything's fine, why do you ask?"

She snaps the case shut, returns it to the table. My stomach hurts as though a big hand has grabbed it and fisted it into a knot.

NANCY ROBARDS THOMPSON   145

"Well, for starters, you haven't returned my calls, and your husband phoned last night after suppertime looking for you and his little girl. Kate, that's not like you."

I walk over to the stove, get the kettle and carry it to the sink. "Oh, well…ummm…we just got our wires crossed."

"Are you and Corbin having problems, baby?"

I turn on the water. "Corbin and I are getting a divorce."

The words spill out in one breath. Just like the water pouring from the faucet. I can't believe I blurt it out when really I had no intention of telling her. Not now. Not in the wake of the news about Dad.

My mother's hand is on my shoulder. The other one reaches out and turns off the tap. She walks me to the table and sits me down, as if I'm five years old.

She sits in the chair next to me, perching on the edge, never once taking her gaze off me. Big, fat, silent tears roll down my face, and I start to shake.

She touches my arm with a gentle hand. "Oh, baby, what's happened?"

I shrug, cover my face with my hands, then let them fall into my lap.

"Is there someone else?"

I nod, sniff and shudder before I say it. "Corbin's having an affair."

All she does is shake her head, wearing that disappointed look that used to slay me when I was a child.

She doesn't believe in divorce. No one in her family has *ever* been divorced. I shouldn't have told her like this.

"I'm sorry," is all I can say, over and over again.

She hugs me. "Now, you just listen to me. You deserve a lot better than this, and if he's cheating, I don't blame you one iota."

That's when the tears really flow. Every drop that's been stopped up inside me since seeing the photos yesterday morning pours out. For my father, for my mother, for my shattered marriage.

This time it's my turn to cry on her shoulder. She strokes my hair and we cry together. I know we'll get through this; I know somehow we will survive this.

Right now, I'm just not quite sure how.

CHAPTER 9

It's the middle of the day, and I don't realize Corbin's home until I turn around on the ladder and see him standing in the middle of the living room. His mouth is open like he wants to say something. Instead, he stands speechless gaping at the walls like a slack-jawed Cro-Magnon man.

I don't care if he hates the tangerine paint or the smell of patchouli in the diffuser. He'll just have to deal with it.

Finally, he manages, "What have you done to our living room?"

Not *Hello* or *How is your day*, just a clipped *What the hell have you done?* enunciated through gritted teeth.

When I was a small girl, my mother used to tell me she couldn't hear me when I forgot my manners. I use the same tactic on him. Except I don't bother to tell him that's what I'm doing. I just ignore him.

I walk over to the diffuser, sprinkle a few more drops of patchouli oil, survey my work.

The paint needs to dry for about an hour before I add the gold wash. Should be ready after I pick up Caitlin from school. Corbin rented a car this morning so transportation isn't a problem today.

Pity. The limo was fun.

"I know you're mad at me," he says. "But have you gone completely off your rocker?"

Hmm...what shall I fix for dinner tonight? Frozen pizza? Corn dogs? Maybe I'll call Enzos and order five-star takeout. Naaaaa, Caitlin would prefer corn dogs.

Maybe I'll get Enzos for me and do a quick corndog for her.

I hum "I am a Rock," contemplate additional dinner possibilities and dab a little patchouli oil on my wrist, behind my ear. Jerk repellent.

"Kate." He grabs my arm, making me drop the open bottle on the carpet as I pull out of his grasp.

"Don't touch me."

He frowns and backs up, both hands in the air. "I got a call today from the store manager at Bloomingdale's thanking me for my purchase of the ten-thousand-dollar Shifman bed. Would you care to explain?"

Oh shit.

I squat down and press the lid back on the paint can. What the hell was the manager doing calling Corbin's office?

The bills go there. Of course.

"I bought a bed. What else would you like to know?"

He crosses his arms and eyes the oily patchouli stain spreading on the floor, rubs his nose and makes a face. "We have a perfectly good bed—"

"That you'll need in your new home." I walk out of the living room to wash the roller in the kitchen sink. He follows me.

"I was hoping it wouldn't come to that," he says.

I glance over my shoulder and see him standing there with his arms akimbo, a defiant stance that suggests he's losing his patience.

"Well, Corbin, I guess you made your bed, didn't you? Now you can take it with you to your new home and lie in it."

Color floods his cheeks. "Whether I stay or go, you are *not* spending ten thousand dollars on a bed."

I drop the roller in the sink and whirl around to face him.

"*You're* not telling me what I can and can't do. If you

want to push someone around, Mel-o-dy would probably like it. She's probably looking for a father figure to
tell her what to do."

He winces. I'd like to believe it was because of the
way I said her name. I'm tempted to keep spitting it at
him, rapid-fire.

Mel-o-dy.

Mel-o-dy.

Mel-o-dy.

Mel-o-dy.

"I said nothing about your limousine excursion yesterday. Nor did I question your shopping spree or mention the way you dumped my five-hundred-dollar
cognac all over the couch during your tantrum."

"Well, you're mentioning it now, so you lose your
gold star on that one."

He rolls his eyes, raises a hand. "You may keep the
diamond necklace I bought you." He pushes the black
velvet box across the table. "But I draw the line at your
spending ten thousand dollars on a bed." He arcs a
brow. "Since you're kicking me out, we're going to have
to tighten our belts if I have to pay for two households."

"As far as I'm concerned, you *should* pay." And *pay
and pay and pay. For the rest of your bloody life.*

I walk to the table and shove the jewelry box back at him. It slides like a lethargic hockey puck.

He smiles—not a nice smile, one I'm sure that's meant to put me in my place. He picks up the jewelry box and puts it in his pocket.

I don't care. He can have it. He'd just better not give it to *her*.

Corbin sighs. "Look, Kate, let's be adult about this."

"Since when have you been interested in adults? Juveniles seem to be more your style these days."

His face is stony, but I can see his jaw tick. "I canceled our Bloomingdale's account and your order for the Shifman. If you want to spend ten thousand dollars on a bed, then I would suggest you get a job."

"Well, that's just fine. *Fine.*" Any store manager stupid enough to call a husband after the wife drops that much money in his store is a moron and doesn't deserve the sale.

I'll show him. I'll call around for the same bed, use a different credit card, and leave strict instructions for the manager not to call my husband because it's a *surprise*.

Corbin turns to leave, but before he does, he glances over his shoulder. "When you start looking for a job, you can rule out interior decorating because the living room looks hideous."

Oh!

"You wait just a minute—" I scream.

He slams the door to the garage.

"Don't you walk out on me!"

I grab the sopping paint roller, yank open the door and fling it at him as hard as I can. It smacks him in the back, leaving a big tangerine-colored splotch on his white shirt.

Corbin's been in his new apartment a week now. He was able to lease a condominium at the Waverly, an up-scale high-rise downtown. The perfect bachelor pad to impress young Mel-o-dy Wentworth, I'm sure.

It's not so bad living here alone with Caitlin.

Really, it's not.

The house is big for two, but it's *our house*. Moving would mean too many changes for her six-year-old mind to process. The counselor agreed. I thought it best to have counseling lined up for when we broke the news.

I know children are resilient, but I want to arm myself with the best resources possible to help her through this. I don't want to scar her for life or have her end up poisoned against marriage as Alex is.

The therapist agreed it would be best if Caitlin could come home to her own familiar surroundings while she gets used to her new room at *Daddy's house*.

The counselor also said it would be best to alert the school to the situation. So they'd understand the changes happening at home.

So you see, this new arrangement really is best for everyone. I can cook when I want to. I can read in bed as late as I want. It's the whole *one less door to answer, one less egg to fry* yada-yada-yada. Though he never knocked on the door. So I guess that part doesn't apply. So I'll replace it with the line in the song that talks about *one less jerk to pick up after*. That rings very true. Living with him was like having another child around the house.

I have so much more time for me now. Time to just sit and think. You know what I realized the other day while I was thinking?

Corbin's been gone a long time. I just wasn't brave enough to admit it. You know how it is. The logical part of your brain warns, *something's wrong*. But your heart clouds the obvious with opaque veiled excuses: *He's quiet because he's tired; he's moody because he's preoccupied with a patient's case*; or any one of the multitude of reasons the heart concocts to blind you to the obvious.

I also realized that not only has *he* been gone a long time. So have I.

The real me, that is. The me I used to be before I lost myself striving to be the perfect wife.

And look where it got me.

It's like this—you dock your boat in the harbor of the American Dream and go on about your business raising a family and making a life just as you thought you always wanted. Somewhere along your well-charted course the woman you used to be jumps ship because you've ignored her needs one too many times taking care of everyone else. You wake up one day and you have no idea who this stranger is staring back at you in the mirror.

Of course it took my marriage breaking up for me to see clearly. But I'm sitting here wondering if it was a gradual chipping away, or was there a decisive moment when the old me said *forget this nonsense* and this stranger stumbled in?

Maybe it happened in the supermarket bread aisle or during a PTA meeting? I know—the genuine me probably checked out when I was cleaning the bathroom. She always hated that chore, seeing how Corbin and Daniel seemed incapable of peeing *in* the toilet.

It's made me take a very long, hard look at myself. Take my hair, for instance. I'm not a natural blonde—as evidenced by these roots that need serious attention.

I walk into the master bath and part my hair and see at least ten wiry grays standing at attention amidst the two-inch row of brown grow-out.

I grab the tweezers and start to yank them out, but I remember Rainey's warning that if you yank out one gray hair, six of its friends will pop in to give it a going-away party.

I groan and toss the tweezers on the bathroom counter.

Maybe I'll start wearing stylish but eccentric hats. I'll become famous around Central Florida as the hat lady.

To fix these roots and the trophy-wife wannabe accessories that go with it—the makeup, the clothing, the toned body—means a lot of time at the salon getting foiled, highlighted, toned, cut and clipped or time working out at the gym or playing tennis.

Oh, and how could I forget the eyebrow, upper lip and bikini waxing?

I'm starting to rethink this whole time-consuming beauty routine. Where did it get me?

Plus, now that Corbin's cut me off, I can't justify slapping down $250 in the salon every six weeks.

I don't have the time or the money.

So forget this *beauty* routine. I'm over it.

No more makeup. No more fussing over the hair.

It's *au naturel* for me.

If I ever date again, the man's going to have to like me for me. Obviously, I'm not cut out for this goddess routine. I can't compete.

Legend says Hera's beauty is renewed each spring and she magically washes away the wear and worry of her immortal lifestyle. I, on the other hand, am not so fortunate.

The stress lines are deeply etched in my face and bags that would accommodate a three-month stay in Europe have taken up permanent residence under my eyes. If most women finally "grow into themselves" at forty, why do I feel as if I've been put out to pasture before I've reached the starting gate?

I'm not even forty yet.

I'm too young to feel this old.

It's raining when I pull into the Liberty School car line, but I still wear my sunglasses and hat. My naked face and shameless roots are securely incognito.

I think I can feel my roots growing as I speak. Will

I wake up one day next week to discover they've taken over the metro Orlando area?

I glance in the rearview mirror to assess the fright factor. Not bad. It's amazing the sins a good pair of sunglasses and a fun hat can hide. This makeup boycott will take some getting used to. Better to let everyone get used to the new, more natural me gradually. Too much at once is a shock to the system.

Not that I'm hung up on what others think—let me rephrase that. I'm *learning* not to be hung up on what others think of me.

When I make it to the head of the car line the rain has eased up. I pull the car alongside the covered walkway where the children wait. Jocelyn Morgan, PTA president, is at her usual post. She spies me, waves and walks over to the passenger-side door. I roll down the window, letting in a blast of rain-humid March air.

Jocelyn braces her forearms on the window frame of my car and leans in. "Hi, Kate. What, no limo today?"

"Nope, you know what they say about too much of a good thing."

"Oh, right." Jocelyn is one of those women who has an annoying habit that I call the *bob and grin*; she nods continuously and maintains an unwavering fake smile throughout your entire conversation, no matter who's speaking. She reminds me of one of those vacant-eyed bobble-head dolls.

"Well, speaking of good things, we're putting together the committees for next year." *Grin. Nod. Nod. Grin. Does the woman blink?*

"We're counting on you to chair the spring carnival again, Kate."

"Why, because no one else is foolish enough to take on the task?"

Quit nodding. You're making me dizzy.

"We didn't ask anyone else because we want *you*, silly."

At least someone does.

"You did such a good job, Kate. This was the best year yet."

"I'll have to think about it and let you know. I'm going back to work."

"Oh right, I heard. I was sorry to hear about your *situation*. Do you need anything?"

She knows? How does she know? I realize I'm digging my nails into my upper arm.

"No, I'm fine, thanks."

"What is it you're doing with yourself now? Limousine service?" She chortles.

I give her my own version of the bob-and-gritted-teeth grin.

I have no idea.

Thank God, Caitlin rolls her backpack to the car and preempts the conversation.

Saved by my darling daughter.

I smile and wave at her. Jocelyn steps back, opens the door and helps her in.

"We're counting on you, Kate." *Grin. Nod. Nod. Grin.*

Oh brother.

After I pull out, I check my rearview mirror. She's already performing the same head-in-the-window routine at the next car.

I feel so special.

Well, good. Let someone else have a turn running the carnival.

"Hi, sweetie. Did you have a nice day?"

Caitlin looks up from buckling her seat belt.

"Jeffery Knight pulled my ponytail."

"Did he?"

"Yes. Mrs. Collins gave him a time-out because he kept pulling it after I told him to stop."

Oh, the strange ways men have of showing their affection begins so young. I consider sharing this with

Caitlin but nix the idea. "It sounds like you handled it exactly as you should have. I'm proud of you."

"Mommy, will you play the *Shrek 2* music?"

I pop in the disk. The random play selects the song, "I Need a Hero."

Caitlin squeals.

Personally, I like the Bonnie Tyler version better than the Fairy Godmother's rendition, but it's still a fun song, especially because it seems to have new meaning now. We sing along until we pull into the Orlando Ballet School parking lot.

I toss the sunglasses and hat in the front seat. Sunglasses outside on a rainy day are one thing, wearing them inside is another. If I'm going to wear this *au naturel* look, I might as well hold my chin up high.

We huddle close together under the big red-and-white golf umbrella as we race inside to get out of the rain.

"Sweetie, while you're in class I'm going to run to the grocery store, okay?"

There are no viewing windows at this school, so parents have to wait in the lobby. I figure I might as well make good use of this time rather than sitting and talking to the other mothers.

"Okay, but you'll be back before I get out of class, right?"

I pull her long hair on top of her head and fashion it into a ballerina bun.

"You can count on it."

Since Corbin and I split, Caitlin's been experiencing some mild separation anxiety. I've never been late picking her up or given her any reason to think I'd leave her stranded. The counselor encourages me to reassure her, says this is normal under these circumstances.

"In fact, you can always reach me on my cell phone. So if anything comes up you call me."

I fasten her bun with extra hairpins and put my hand over her eyes to shield them from the generous dose of hairspray I use to tame her wispy tendrils.

"What might come up?" She scowls. She looks so much like her father when she makes that expression. The pang sneaks up on me.

"Nothing will come up, but I just want you to know you can reach me any time you need me."

She's quiet as I finish tucking under a few stray fly-aways. I kneel down in front of her.

"Have fun?"

"Okay." She hugs me, then runs her hands over my cheeks. "You look pretty today, Mommy."

"Thank you." I plant a kiss on her nose and whisper a silent prayer of thanks for this little angel.

I don't bother to don the hat and glasses in Publix Supermarket.

I don't need them.

I feel good about me.

No, I feel great.

I hold my head up high as I search for the things I need.

Grocery shopping is so much easier now. I've always enjoyed preparing nice meals. But now that it's just Caitlin and me, I can make things that Corbin would turn his nose up at—like salads as a main course.

It's actually less trouble to fix two different dinners for Caitlin and me than it was to fix the elaborate meals Corbin expected.

Dinner is much less stressed when all I have to do is heat a can of SpaghettiOs in the microwave and serve baby carrots with a side of ranch dressing.

The most gratifying part is Caitlin would choose Chef Boyardee over my beef Wellington any day.

I'm thrilled.

I may have changed the fare, but there are two things I will always insist upon: that Caitlin and I sit down at the table together for at least one meal a day; and I will grocery shop everyday. I'm a stickler for freshness, and I enjoy the process. It's very European.

I grab some chicken—chicken tenders tonight for Caitlin; chicken salad for me—a bag of mixed baby greens, a couple of tomatoes and a fresh loaf of bread. That should hold us until tomorrow.

I pay for my purchases, check my watch as I walk to my car. I have enough time to grab a mocha at the Starbucks on the corner and make it back to retrieve my daughter.

Who needs complicated meals when you can appreciate the simple things in life?

I guess a ten-thousand-dollar bed isn't exactly simple. I actually feel a little foolish having gone to such great lengths to get it. But I proved my point to Corbin.

Point-proving doesn't make for a simple life, says Hera.

That's one of the big differences between Corbin and me. With him everything has to be so…so convoluted and complicated.

Give me the simple pleasures in life any day. That's what makes me happy. Things like the golden light that filters through my favorite oak tree in our neighbor's backyard at twilight; the way the air smells in the fall; the sound of sharp scissors cutting paper; or even more than that—the sound of Caitlin's belly laugh when she's really tickled; old movies; hot baths; candlelight; the crispy cheese on the bottom of a piece of pizza; the way the blooms on my camellia bush remind me of ballerina tutus; the sound of a cat purring. Corbin hates cats.

Maybe Caitlin and I will go to the Humane Society and get a cat this weekend.

Perhaps we'll get two.

We could name them Hera and Zeus.

If we love him enough, maybe this time, Zeus will learn to be faithful.

As I approach my car, I see a flat back tire.

And the rain comes down.

•

CHAPTER 10

Perfect.

Just perfect.

This is *not* on the list of things I love.

I wring my hands, then toe the listless, sagging rubber caught under the wheel like a piece of flabby skin.

I put my groceries in the car, then sit in the driver's seat to look for my American Automobile Association card.

Found it.

I punch the toll-free number into my cell phone and sit there while it rings.

A perky voice greets me and takes my member number.

"I'm sorry, your Triple A membership expired six months ago."

What is this, karmic payback for wrecking Corbin's car?

I tap the useless red, white and blue card on the

steering wheel and vaguely recall Corbin mentioning he wasn't going to renew it because Beck's, the garage where he takes the cars, offers roughly the same services at a substantial discount. That's because Jon Beck is a friend of ours.

Sometimes Corbin can be so damned cheap it kills me.

So now what?

I don't want to call Beck's because it would mean talking to Jon and that would mean explaining why I was calling instead of Corbin—

Why did Corbin always call? asks Hera.

Because it's a man's job.

I did the girl jobs. He did the manly jobs.

Why are you always expecting someone to come running to your rescue? You've got to learn to help yourself before anyone else can help you. Dependency's what got you into this mess in the first place.

Dependency? That's ridiculous. In case you haven't noticed, *I'm* the one who takes care of everyone else.

Maybe so, but you've got to learn to take care of yourself, too, and this is a fine place to start.

Yeah, don't start with me. I'm not in the mood.

Hera laughs.

"I'll show you who's taking care of whom...."

Well, you'd better get to it.

I glance at the dashboard clock. I have about forty-five minutes before I have to get Caitlin.

My stomach clenches.

There aren't too many things that rattle me, but one of them is when something stands between me getting to my child. I was the same way with Daniel when he was little.

If I say I'm going to be somewhere at a certain time, I'm there.

The last thing Caitlin needs right now is to stand there, wondering if her mother left, too.

Calm down. Think logically. It's not brain surgery... says Hera.

Or orthopedic surgery...like Corbin does every day.

Just change the tire. It can't be that hard.

I open the glove compartment and pull out the owner's manual, flip to the page that shows how step-by-step.

For a second I feel as if my head might implode. I rub my temples trying to get some relief.

I don't have time for the indulgence of self-pity. I suck it up and get out and get ready to work, resisting the urge to give the mangled tire a swift kick. And oh, how I want to kick it—good and hard—but at this rate, if I do, I'd probably break my foot.

I use the remote on my key chain to pop the trunk latch, swipe the back of my hand across my damp forehead and contemplate the empty trunk.

Now what?

I glance at the owner's manual for a hint.

Following a hunch, I pull up on a silver loop and the carpet lining the trunk lifts.

A car whizzed past, its tires spraying water.

"Here goes," I mumble and lift the flooring that covers the wheel well and pull out the lug nut wrench.

As in the manual diagrams, I place the jack under the side of the car and pump the back left of the Lexus off the ground. Ha! Like I actually know what I'm doing.

My anxiety eases into a smug amazement.

"I can do this," I murmur. "No sweat."

Ha ha! Just goes to show you—I fit the wrench over one of the nuts—the more you stew over something— I nudge it, but nothing happens, so I lean on it harder— the bigger and uglier the job becomes— I grunt and lean my full weight into it—until it's totally blown out of—

The wrench slips.

The tool bounces off the car, and I stumble and knock my head against the wheel well.

"Ouch! Oh, *come on!* Why is this so hard?"

I get right back in there, line up the wrench and give it another good, hard turn.

It slips again, but this time I'm smart enough to jump away from the car and escape the head blow, but I score another ding in the paint.

A man gets into the Jetta next to me. He cranks the engine and pulls out.

"No thanks! Don't worry about it. I don't need any help. Thanks for asking."

Okay, this isn't as easy as I'd hoped. But there's got to be a way.

There's always a way.

I squat next to the wheel and notice the deep scrapes rounding off the edges of the nut. If I keep this up, I'll strip them.

Time for plan B.

If I had a plan B.

I stand and glance around, notice a service station on the southwest corner. Perfect.

I get in and drive to the station at a snail's pace. The

air-conditioning feels good, dissipating some of the sticky humidity.

I pull right up in front of the garage portion of the station. Get out and flash my best smile at the two grease monkeys working under a lift.

"Excuse me...ummm... Hi, I'm hoping you could help me. I have a flat tire and I tried to change it myself, but I can't seem to get the nuts off—"

The younger of the two men laughs.

"I got the same problem, lady."

Oh. It dawns on me what I just said. What he just said. My hand flies to my collar.

Oh, grow up.

The pervert disappears inside the office. Through the open door, I can see him sit down behind the desk and make a phone call.

The other man hasn't as much as taken his eyes off the underbelly of the car he's working on.

"Excuse me," I say again. "Can you change my tire for me?"

"Lady, I got a four-hour backup here." He talks out of the side of his mouth.

"I can get to you about eleven o'clock tomorrow. If you want to come back."

"But it's only a flat tire."

"Yeeeeeeeep."

He still hasn't looked at me.

He has black grime under his nails and dirt caked in the creases of his sweaty neck.

From the intense way he scowls and bites his bottom lip as he does whatever it is he's doing to the car, I suspect he's a man who does not possess a sense of humor nor compassion for a woman who must pick up her child in half an hour.

I don't like him.

I drive back across the street to the Publix parking lot. The car pulls hard to the side. It's pouring now, making the street slick and hard to navigate. Any thoughts I entertained about driving back to Orlando Ballet on this flat go out the window.

I pull into a parking place and curse the two *lug nuts* who wouldn't help me.

Now for plan C.

I dial information. "Beck's Garage, please."

"I have a listing for Beck's Automotive on Mills Ave."

"Yes, that's it."

"I'll be happy to connect you."

"Thank you."

"Beck's Automotive. Jon Beck speaking."

"John, hi, this is Kate Hennessey. How are you?"

"Hey, Kate. I'm doing great. It's good to hear from you."

There's something comforting in his Southern drawl. But I still brace myself for the inevitable, *How's that husband of yours*. Much to my relief, he doesn't ask.

I know better than to ask him about Pam. They divorced a couple of years ago.

We used to get together occasionally, the four of us. Pam's a nurse. Works with Corbin at the hospital. After she introduced Corbin and Jon, Corbin started taking our cars to Beck's.

She left Jon for a pediatrician. It's been a good two and a half years since I've seen him.

"I'm in a bit of a bind and I was hoping you could help me. I'm at the College Park Publix, and I have a flat tire. I tried to change it myself—"

"Do you have a spare?"

"Yes."

"Say no more. I'll be there in seven minutes."

I had forgotten how handsome Jon was.

Tall—probably six-four; longish light brown hair;

great smile, with lots of straight, white teeth. He looks a lot like the actor John Corbett. I've always thought so.

How could Pam give him up?

Foolish woman.

But he's not *my* type. Especially as I watch him unfold his lanky self out of his truck; a khaki rain slicker worn open over a Harley Davidson T-shirt and a pair of old faded Levi's. I'd wager they're the 501 button-fly variety, but—well, I can't bring myself to look to be sure. I mean, this is *Jon*.

Pretty Pam's Jon.

Pretty Pam's ex-Jon.

I squeeze the umbrella handle and my eyes meander south.

Bingo. Button fly.

"Kate, it's good to see you, darlin'. It's been too long." He pulls me into a hug. He smells good. Not how you'd think a mechanic would smell. A mixture of woodsy green and Dial soap.

Reflected in the truck's windshield, I catch a distorted glimpse of myself in his arms: my cheeks are hollow and drawn; my eyes are two empty caverns; my dark roots disappear into the windshield making the blond portion seem to dance an inch away from my scalp in a humidity-induced riot of waves.

I look like Picasso's interpretation of Medusa.

Uggh. I step away from Jon.

"I don't mean to rush you, but I have to pick up Caitlin in ten minutes."

I'm wringing my hands again and clasp them together to make myself stop.

Hera stands behind Jon with her arms crossed, frowning. *That was rude. He rides to your rescue like the cavalry in a tow truck and this is how you show your gratitude? Come on, girlfriend. Didn't you learn anything in your Junior League years? Be gracious. Be—*

"Where is she?" he says.

"At Orlando Ballet, across from Lake Ivanhoe."

He glances at his watch.

"Get in the truck. We'll go get her. Then I'll change your tire. Sound like a plan?"

I am so relieved I want to hug him all over again. But I don't. I grab my purse off the passenger seat, and the hat and glasses. As he walks around to the driver's side, I twist my hair up under the cap, shove the glasses on and climb in the truck.

Forget the cavalry. As far as I'm concerned, Jon Beck

is a knight in shining armor; the slightly rusted tow truck is his noble steed.

"How old is Caitlin now?" he asks as he turns left onto Edgewater Drive.

"She turned six in September."

"That's right, she and Molly are the same age."

"How is Molly?"

"She's living with her mother. She's doing all right."

His voice does an upturn on the words *all right*. It makes him seem like an overgrown boy whose voice is trying to catch up with his gangly body. I want to reach out and squeeze his hand, tell him I understand and that everything *will* be all right.

But I don't know if it will be.

He's been at this two years now. Corbin and I haven't even filed for divorce yet. How would I know whether everything will be all right?

"What was the hardest part?" I ask.

He slants me a glance, and I wish I hadn't asked. It's a nosy question. He'd be within his rights to tell me to mind my own business.

He pulls to a stop at the red light, cocks his head to the left, looks up at my sun visor, then at me.

"Coming home to an empty house." He shrugs,

looks away. "Even though it was just the three of us, the house used to be so full of life. Good smells coming from the kitchen, the dog barking, the television blaring. Sometimes the chaos used to drive me nuts. Now, it all seems dead."

The light turns green. He accelerates slow and steady, just like his Southern drawl.

"Corbin moved out."

Jon checks his side-view mirror, changes lanes, then looks at me again. "Sorry. When did it happen?"

"Last month."

I'm pulled out to sea by a rip current of embarrassment. That Jon might think my call for help is a well-orchestrated ploy to see him because I'm free and he's free and…it feels wrong and awkward.

I know Jon, but I don't really know him beyond our occasional dinners that stopped as abruptly as they started. It was Corbin and Pam who had everything in common: hospital politics; innovations in health care; a certain chemistry that might have made me jealous had I gotten jealous in those days.

Jon and I were the indulging spouses along for the ride…. Oh, God. Could we have been that blind? It's so obvious now—why else would Mr. Above It All have had a social interest in a nurse and an auto mechanic?

"I tried to change the tire myself, but I couldn't get the bolts off, so I drove it to the service station across the street, but they couldn't work me in until tomorrow, so I—"

"You didn't drive on it flat like that, did you?" He frowns.

"What?" I'm so busy inwardly cringing and trying to think of what to say to prove I didn't call him to compare divorce notes that it takes me a minute to understand what he's saying. "Well, yes. I had to get the car across the street. And back again."

"I hope you didn't bend the wheel rim."

"Uh-oh."

Sitting next to Jon—out of context, without Corbin and Pam—I feel cut wide-open. Naked and—

"I think feeling so vulnerable is the hardest part for me. I don't like being vulnerable."

"Sucks, doesn't it?"

He reaches out and squeezes my hand—nothing inappropriate or flirtatious—just a gesture that says, I hear you.

CHAPTER 11

Saturday at noon, Rainey and Alex are waiting for me in a corner booth at The Blue Armadillo. It's a kitschy hole-in-the-wall with a jukebox that plays non-stop Elvis tunes. It also serves the best Tex-Mex in Central Florida and margaritas that go down easy and leave you feeling no pain.

The place is decorated with strings of chili pepper lights, tacky sombreros and blue armadillo piñatas. It's in such bad taste you have to love it.

The girls wave when they see me.

"Look at you." Rainey hugs me. "You look terrific."

Which translates to, *You don't look like you've been through hell and back this month.* The Chanel sunglasses are *terrific*, but the rest is standard Kate. Copper Capri pants and sleeveless black mock turtleneck.

"Rah-rah. How was the football game?" Alex waves an imaginary pompon.

"Uggggggh. It went into overtime." I sit down, tuck my sunglasses in my purse. Rainey pours me a margarita from the pitcher they ordered. "Thank you. I need this. I love my daughter, but this cheerleading thing is for the birds."

I sip my drink and help myself to a tortilla chip and artichoke dip. Elvis's "Heartbreak Hotel" starts up on the jukebox.

I don't even have to look at them to know what they're thinking. That my newfound aversion to Caitlin's extracurricular activity stems from my loathing of Mel-o-dy Wentworth. But I'm not going there. Not yet anyway. I just got *here*. I need a couple more 'ritas before I can discuss her.

"Thank God the season's over in three weeks. I don't think I can take much more. Who ever heard of football in the spring anyway? It's a fall sport."

"That bad?" says Rainey.

I nod.

"I saw that one coming a mile away." Alex rolls her eyes and bites into a chip. "Why'd you let her do it in the first place? Do you really think it's a healthy image for a little girl? Standing on the sidelines, cheering on the boys. Come on boys, you can do it. But all I can do is stand here and wave my pompoms."

I know where she's going with this.

"Oh, come off it, Alex. It's something all little girls need to try on for size."

She snorts. "I was never a cheerleader."

"Exactly," says Rainey. "Look at you."

I change the subject.

"It's not the six-year-olds who are so bad. It's the adults. There's this one woman—I swear, it's like she stepped off of the set of a *Saturday Night Live* skit."

They sip their drinks, waiting.

"Picture a ponytailed, heavyset woman, about forty. Got it?"

They nod.

"She spends the entire game prancing up and down the sidelines crowing about how much *spirit* the girls have, then starts demonstrating her own spirit level. She actually fell in line with the girls and cheered with them. Six-year-old cheerleaders are cute, but we're talking a forty-year-old peewee football cheerleader wannabe. It's just wrong."

"You're serious." Alex eyes me then Rainey. "She's

NANCY ROBARDS THOMPSON   181

serious. I'm glad I wasn't there. I would have been forced to kill her."

"Who is she?" asks Rainey.

"One of the parents."

"Fulfilling her unrequited fantasies at the expense of her daughter," says Rainey. "I pity that child."

"Honey, in her mind she's one of the squad," says Alex.

"I shouldn't be talking like this. Caitlin's having a good time. It's helping draw her out of her shell."

"You have every right to talk like this." Alex munches on a chip. "There's something inherently wrong with a middle-aged woman acting like that, and it gives us license to mock her—mercilessly."

"How's your dad doing?" Rainey asks.

"He's feeling a little stronger. That chemo is brutal. We're in a holding pattern right now."

"How's your mother handling all this?" Alex asks.

"I really think she's in denial. I try to get her to talk about things, but she won't hear of it. I don't mean to be heartless. I mean, I don't want to face the facts, either. But the reality is she's never been alone since they got married almost fifty years ago. It's going to be a real adjustment for her if something happens. She'll have to move in with me."

I shrug.

"Mom and Dad came to the game."

"Was Corbie-baby there?" When Alex calls him that, she always uses a voice that reminds me of Bert on *Sesame Street*.

I shake my head. "I dropped Caitlin off at his place on the way over here."

Rainey leans in. "What's it like?"

I shrug. "Haven't seen it yet. He met me outside." I take a big gulp of my drink.

"Was *she* there?"

I can tell Rainey's been dying to ask about Mel-o-dy since I walked in the room. I had to give her credit for holding off this long.

"Of course not. Caitlin's spending the day with him. She'd better not be there."

"Have you outlined that?" asked Alex.

"I shouldn't have to outline it. He knows what's good for his child."

Alex and Rainey exchange a glance.

"You're giving him a lot of credit," says Rainey.

"Kate, I'd suggest you be very specific in what you want and what you don't, unless you want to be surprised."

I refill my glass, and I decide I can't hold out any

longer. I reach in my bag and pull out exhibit A. I slide the envelope across the table.

Rainey holds up her hands as if she's afraid to touch it. "Is this…?"

I sneer and nod. "Go ahead and look. Don't worry. It's not contagious."

Alex chuckles. "It's not funny. It's just that I can't believe you brought them."

The server, a young guy dressed like a mariachi, steps up to the table, flirts with Rainey, who is too busy peeking into the envelope to notice. He eventually stops trying to be cute and takes our orders.

I lose my appetite watching disgust wash over Rainey's face; I wonder if the guy thinks he provoked that reaction in his sombrero with its black and red balls dangling from the brim. Naaaa, he probably thinks he's Zorro. *More power to you, Zorro.* I order my usual cheese enchilada and taco plate with refried beans and yellow rice.

When we're alone again, Rainey pulls out the photos, flips through them one by one.

My cell phone rings "Jingle Bells." Caitlin's changed it again. She's probably calling me just to laugh about changing the ring. I don't recognize the number on the LCD screen.

Oh, I miss her already.

"Hello, cutie-pie. I've been expecting you to call."

Dead silence on the other end of the line.

"Well, if I would have known that, I'd have called a lot sooner," says a bemused voice. I close my eyes and clasp my hand over my mouth. I know that deep Southern drawl.

"Kate?" he says again.

I open my eyes. Rainey and Alex look as though they're about to climb over the table and perform CPR. I wave them off.

"Hi, Jon. Yes, I'm here. Slightly mortified, but…I was expecting someone else."

"Jon? Who's Jon?" They look at me, at each other.

I put my finger to my lips.

"Ouch," he says. "Shot through the heart. It was the first time I'd been called a cutie-pie. Well, lucky guy, this cutie-pie."

I laugh. "I was expecting Caitlin."

"Okay, that's better. She definitely qualifies for cutie-pie status."

"Yes, she does."

Alex or Rainey, I don't know who, kicks me under the table. "Who's Jon?"

I pointedly turn away because I've already made a buffoon out of myself once, and I'm having a hard enough time focusing without them distracting me.

"Who's Jon?"

I kick someone. Hard.

"Owwwww!" It was Rainey.

I mouth *sorry*, get up and walk to the front of the restaurant as the first strains of "Love Me Tender" begin. Don't want to be one of those inconsiderate cell phone users who talks too loud and spoils everyone else's meal.

"Is that Elvis?"

"It is. I'm at The Blue Armadillo with some girlfriends."

"Well, then I won't keep you. I was just calling to say thanks for the brownies you dropped off yesterday. They were delicious. How'd you know they're my favorite?"

I walk outside and settle on the cement bench, grateful for the liquid courage from the two margaritas I downed before he called.

"I'm glad you liked them. You did save my life. It was either brownies or be indebted to you forever."

I cringe. *Why did I say that?*

"Hmm… I may have to reconsider that offer. Wow,

this is a day of firsts. Called a cutie-pie and got an offer of lifetime indebtedness—I think there still might
be a few crumbs left. May I exchange the brownies?"

"Nope, sorry. No returns. No exchanges."

Hera whispers, *Look at you, girlfriend. Holding your own.*

"I was afraid of that," he says.

There's an awkward pause on the line.

"Really, Jon, thanks for everything. You did save
my life."

"All in a day's work, darlin'."

My stomach does a little two-step. I place my hand
on my belly because I shouldn't be getting all warm and
twittery over an old friend calling me *darlin'*. Even
though I like the way his Southern accent rounds off
the edges of the word.

"Kate, would you like to get together sometime?"

This time my stomach does a complete backflip, and
I sit up straight.

"I'm sure Caitlin would love to see Molly again. That
would be nice."

Hera plants her hands on her curvy hips. *Weenie. You
know damn good and well that's not what he meant.*

I am not even divorced yet. I can't date.

Darlin', you can do anything your little heart desires.

Too bad there's not a place for me to run and hide from *you*.

Hera just smiles.

"Is Caitlin out of school a week from Monday? Molly is. It's a teacher workday or something like that."

"She is."

"How about if we take a late-night trip to the beach a week from tomorrow? There's a lunar eclipse and Molly and I were going to pack a picnic supper, load up the telescope, head on over to Cocoa."

"Oh, Jon, no. I don't want to intrude on your time with her."

"She'd much rather have a friend along than spend the evening with her old man. And we can stay out late because the girls don't have to get up early for school on Monday. And have you ever seen a lunar eclipse? It's magnificent. It's like nature is pulling a copper-colored shade over the moon. It'll take your breath away."

I swallow hard. "All right, you sold me. As long as you're sure we won't be intruding."

"Not a chance. We'll pick you up at four o'clock, okay?"

An anxious mix of hope and discontent brews inside me, repelling each other like two positively charged magnets forced together. Only hope and discontent are about as opposite as two emotions can be.

Actually, the more I think about it, the more it feels as if I've ventured out to the edge of a high diving board, and I'm contemplating a jump.

I watch the cars whiz by on the street in front of the restaurant, recall how much I hate high dives. When I was a little girl, we used to go to this public pool to swim in the summertime. Once, I waited in a long line that stretched from the lounge chairs all the way up the ladder of the high dive so I could jump off. When it was finally my turn, I couldn't do it. The sun was beating down on me, the water was sparkling so bright that it hurt my eyes—it looked too shallow to jump—and the kids were yelling at me because I was taking so long.

I turned around and pushed past all of them waiting on the ladder and climbed back down to the ground.

I've always preferred to have my feet on the ground. That way I can gauge exactly how deep the water is before I take the plunge.

CHAPTER 12

I wish I could walk into Borders and buy a book called Guidelines for Divvying up a Twenty-year Marriage: What to do with half a life's-worth of discarded memories.

There is no such book in print.

Maybe I'll write it someday.

"Rainey, I need to get a job." She's come over to help me paint the bedroom Scarlett O'Hara. She stops rolling on red paint and gives me this horror-stricken look.

"I'm okay with it. I'm not above working for a living. I know I'll get a decent settlement. But for my own peace of mind, I need more to look forward to in life than alimony and child support checks."

I come from a working-class family. My mother never worked outside the home, but it wouldn't have hurt if she had. In fact, it would have been a good thing.

She'd be less dependent on my father now and money wouldn't have been so tight. But my father had his pride. So my mother depended on her man and perfected the art of stretching a dollar.

We didn't have the finest things, like Corbin's family, but we never went hungry.

"Is Corbin on your case about it?"

I nod and peel off another piece of border from the wall that abuts the ceiling. "If you could have heard him last night when he brought Caitlin home, you'd think we were one step away from the poor farm. Of course it didn't help that he'd discovered that I circumvented him and bought that bed. He'll never let me forget it."

Rainey laughs, sets down her paint roller and plops down on the bed. "I have to admit, I'm having a hard time understanding how a bed could be worth ten thousand dollars."

She bounces a little.

I let a long piece of border fall to the ground. "Whose side are you on?"

"Yours, of course." She sits up, runs her hand over the mattress top. "I'm not saying you shouldn't have done it. I'm just saying I don't see how anyone can make one bed worth ten thousand dollars."

"Go to their Web site. They explain it beautifully. But I'm not keeping the bed."

"What? You're not sending it back, are you?"

I shake my head. "I've made my point to Corbin. So I'm giving it to my parents. Mom said Dad's having trouble sleeping. This bed is like sleeping on a cloud. I thought maybe it would help him."

"Wow, that's really a nice thing to do."

I shrug. "I just wish a bed could make him well."

Rainey gets up and resumes painting. We work in silence for a while. I've found that as with divorce, cancer talk often renders people mute. I break the ice.

"You should have seen Corbin. He was on the warpath last night. He wanted to sit down and outline everything right then—which days he'd get to see Caitlin, how much money he'd give me per month, the furniture and CDs he'd take. He said, 'I have to plan, you know. I'm not footloose and fancy-free like you are.'"

"Oh give me a break."

"Yep, that's me. Just call me Ms. 'Blowin' in the Wind.'"

"I'll bet you wanted to smack him."

"Oh, I am way beyond that. For the first time in my life I've started thinking about hitting him where it really hurts."

"Oooooh, going for the old bank account jugular."

I climb down from the ladder and gather the pieces of stripped border into a pile. "I have never thought that way before, but he started it. He assured me he'd provide adequately for his daughter and cover Daniel's tuition, but then he got all funny about what I wanted. Like I was going to try to rob him. You know, at this point, I don't even know what I want. I haven't even come to terms with the extra drawer space he left when he moved out. So I certainly haven't had a chance to figure out what I want to fill it with."

Rainey pours more paint into the pan. "He was just in a mood."

"Well, he made it exceedingly clear that money is going to be an issue between us. I can't blame him for getting angry over the bed. But I don't make a habit of doing things like that, and he knows it. After twenty years, he'd better not think he can skate on out of here *footloose and fancy-free*."

"I guess it's expensive to have a girlfriend and pay alimony and child support."

"Yes, which brings up another issue. I told him I didn't want his girlfriend there when Caitlin visits."

Rainey nods. "That's fair. And as I said, you need to spell it out."

"You know what he says? 'I'm not going to do anything that's going to hurt *my* daughter.' All I can say is he'd better not try to take Caitlin away from me. If he's afraid of things getting ugly…"

Rainey looks at me through narrowed eyes. "I'm sure he won't do that."

I sit on the edge of the bed. "I don't know, Rainey. I'm scared. You should have seen him. He's the one making all the money. I don't even have a job. If he marries that bimbo and tries to take away my baby—"

My voice catches. Rainey comes over and sits on the bed next to me. "Hey, come on. He's not going to do that."

She squeezes my hand and smirks. "If he brings a kid into the house, then he can't screw the bimbo on the kitchen counter."

My mouth falls open.

"Gee, thanks, Rain. Is that supposed to make me feel better?"

"No, it's supposed to make you see how things really are. You are a smart, capable woman. If you're afraid he's going to try and take Caitlin away from you, start training for the fight now. What kind of job do you want?"

What to do with myself outside the role of mother and wife? The thought is almost overwhelming. It's been a long time since I held a job outside the home.

"My degree's in interior design. I worked as a decorator a year-and-a-half to support us while Corbin was in medical school." After he graduated, we agreed I'd quit to take care of the kids. I didn't mind. Call me unambitious if you must, but what's wrong with wanting to make a nice home?

"Of course. You're a natural. People are always asking you for advice. You've kept up with the latest interior fashions and trends—like your hot Moroccan living room."

I laugh.

"The hair on the back of Corbin's neck stood up when he saw it with the gold overwash and the tapestry-covered ceiling. It was priceless."

"In fact, I may have a lead for you. You know the new museum they're building downtown? Marilyn Griggs, the executive director, mentioned that she's interviewing designers. I could see if she'd talk to you."

A knot forms in the pit of my stomach. Just as it's been a long time since I held a job outside the home, it's been just as long since I've interviewed or talked to clients. I don't even have a current portfolio.

Oh come on, says Hera. *Don't you go tossing around those lame excuses. Get your act together and draw some renderings, put together some mock-up boards.*

I think about it for a minute. Yes, this might work. It will be good for Caitlin to see her mother stand on her own two feet for a change.

"That would be great."

"So tell me about this enigmatic Jon who called last week during lunch."

The way my knotted stomach unfurls and spirals at the mention of his name is disturbing.

"He's just an old friend. Our mechanic. He has a daughter, Molly, who's Caitlin's age."

Rainey's not buying it. I turn away from her so I don't have to endure the incredulous looks she's throwing at me.

"He's a great guy, but I have way too much going on to add a great guy to the mix."

Even though I'm not looking at her, I feel her dubious glances land like darts in my back.

"Okay, fine." I turn to her. "Caitlin and I are going to the beach with him and Molly."

Her eyes brighten, then her face falls.

"Uggggh, bathing suit on the first date?"

"It's *not* a date. We're getting the girls together."

She gives me an *oh get off it* look.

I shake my head. "It's not a date. I just… I just can't. Sometimes I think I have it all figured out. It should be cut and dried—Corbin cheated. He's out. But sometimes the pendulum swings so far back in the other direction I catch myself looking for ways to justify what he did."

I swallow hard.

"Sometimes I want to ask him to come home. Because I'm still not sure I can initiate the divorce."

She hugs me and I cry.

"We called Daniel last night and told him. That made it real. I guess I thought that until we told him there was a chance. But this morning when I woke up I was thinking the last time Daniel was home we were a family. Now we're…" I swipe at my tears. "God, what are we? I'm not sure anymore."

Sunday morning, I'm sitting at the kitchen table drinking my second cup of coffee and reading the want ads, when the chain saw starts.

I don't think much of it at first—just someone's Sunday morning yard work. It's the earthshaking thud that makes me get up and look out the window.

I see a man in a white T-shirt scaling the trunk of
the huge oak tree I love so much in my neighbor's yard.

"They're not—"

Oh my God, they are. They're cutting down *my* tree.

Technically it's not mine, but I've had a love affair with that tree since the day we moved into this
house.

As the man in white slices off another piece of trunk
I feel as if I'm watching an old friend being torturously
dismembered. I want to scream; I want to weep from the
atrocity of it.

I bang on the window, but he can't hear me over the
obnoxious roar. "Stop! Stop it!"

I cover my face and peek through my fingers.

They must have started this butchery yesterday. I was
out all day—they've already taken off the branches.
All the lush green leaves are gone. The trunk is all
that's left. It stands erect like a thirty-foot middle finger at full salute.

The guy in the white T-shirt has crampons on his
feet and a red safety harness around his waist. It's a horrific sight watching him up there. Like David scaling
Goliath and attacking him with a chain saw.

"What's wrong, Mommy?" Caitlin calls from upstairs.

"Nothing, sweetie, they're just cutting down the tree next door, and I don't want them to."

She comes running downstairs and looks out the window. "Can't you make them stop?"

Yeah, don't just stand there, says Hera. *Do something.*

Like what? Even if I wanted to do something, it's too late now. They've already... Oh, they've already killed it.

So you're just going to stand here and let them do it. Hera shakes her head.

I open the back door and go outside. Caitlin follows. I hear my neighbors' voices above the saw and walk around to the front of the house. Jane and Carl Carter are out in the driveway standing next to their bright yellow Hummer, dressed in their Sunday best. They're both shading their eyes looking up at the tree murderers.

"Jane? Carl? Why are you cutting down the tree? Is it diseased?" Caitlin hangs on my leg.

Carl shakes his head, straightens his tie. "No. Last year when hurricane Charley blew through, it dropped a few branches. You remember. A real nuisance."

A nuisance? Is that what it boils down to? When something inconveniences you, just cut it down? You don't just cut down an old tree like that.

Hera says, *Whoa, don't go getting all uppity, Ms. High*

and Mighty. Isn't that exactly what you did to Corbin? Cut him off at the knees just because he dropped an indiscreet branch where he shouldn't have? You didn't give him a chance.

"But it was a perfectly fine tree. Do you know how old it was? Do you know how long it takes for those old oaks to grow like that?"

Jane tucks her Bible under her arm, opens the passenger side door. "You'll be thanking us come next hurricane season. Your perfectly fine tree might just fall on our house. Or yours. Better to get rid of it now and cut our losses."

My perfectly fine tree? No, if it were my perfectly fine tree we wouldn't be having this conversation.

The roar of the chain saw flares. Caitlin plugs her ears. Carl yells above the noise, "It had to go. I have a family to protect."

Instinctively, my arms encircle Caitlin, who is leaning on me, her back against the front of my legs, looking up at the tree man.

Well… I had a family.

And we loved this tree.

If Corbin were here, this wouldn't be happening. We used to watch the sunset over that tree. We'd mar-

vel at the way the light shone the most brilliant shades of gold and amber through the leaves and branches.

"Have you ever seen anything more beautiful?" I said once.

He put his arms around me and kissed me. "I'm looking at her."

A portion of the tree trunk breaks free and falls. The ground shakes.

I bite my lip until it throbs. I feel the dam of tears rising, threatening to overflow.

"But—" my voice cracks "—you can't replace… trees like that."

The chain saw blares. I swipe at my tears, cover my ears.

Jane and Carl exchange an uneasy glance.

"Have to run." Jane mouths the words and gives a little wave before she climbs into the car.

"Excuse us, Kate, we don't want to be late for church."

Carl gets behind the wheel of that big, ugly yellow Hummer and drives away.

Tears stream down my face.

I'm sure Jane and Carl are rolling their eyes and saying terrible things like *No wonder Corbin left her.*

He didn't leave. I *made* him leave.

Exactly. Hera cocks a brow, makes a sound like a

chain saw. *Cut that twenty-year marriage right down. You threw him out without even trying to fix things. No marriage counseling, no nothing. Cut him loose right into Mel-o-dy Wentworth's arms. Happy now?*

Do I look happy?

I see two birds circling high above the tree. It was probably their home. I know how they feel. And I still have my home.

"Mommy? Don't cry." Caitlin hugs my legs and I sink down to my knees and bury my face in her blond curls and sob like a child.

"Let's go in the house," she says, way too grown-up for a six-year-old. As she takes me by the hand and leads me, I know right then that I can't let this go any further. I have to do something to make this right.

I'm throwing away twenty years of marriage over one mistake? A big mistake, granted, but is it something we can't overcome with marriage counseling?

To save our family?

I go into the kitchen, pick up the phone, start to dial, then stop.

Caitlin comes into the room trailing a fistful of toilet paper. Wipes my tears and gives me another hug. Then leaves the room.

No, I will not let our family fall apart.

I dial Corbin's new phone number.

I pace the kitchen floor, and in my mind's eye I glimpse our future. This time next year we'll be sitting at the kitchen table, sipping coffee and eating my homemade cinnamon rolls late on a lazy Sunday morning much like this—only no obnoxious chain saws buzzing. He'll reach out and take my hand and say, "I'm so glad you didn't give up on me."

And we'll look at each other and know how far we've come and how much stronger we are because of it.

"Hello?"

Hearing his voice floods me with the kind of relief you get when you know you've made the right choice; when your little lifeboat survives the storm and you know you have a distance yet to travel, but you're going home again.

"Corbin, the Carters cut down our tree."

I wait for him to connect with me, to get as indignant over the atrocity as I am.

"What? Oh, hi." His voice sounds flat, distracted. Probably just nervous.

"Come home," I say, wanting him to know it's going to be okay. "I want to talk about this."

Then I hear what sounds like little-girl laughter in

the background. "Who's that?" the babyish voice says. "Don't make Melody come over there and find out for herself—"

The phone goes mute as if he's put his hand over the mouthpiece.

My blood goes cold.

Oh, God! *She's* there.

I flatten my back against the wall and listen to the muffled mumbling in the background.

I don't want to listen, but I can't make myself hang up.

He lifts the phone mute, "Let me call you back."

The line goes dead.

I stare at the phone.

Shit.

Oh. My. God. She was there. At his place. I guess I should have known she'd be there. Of course. He's free to see who he wants.

Still, this hurts worse than seeing the pictures.

Because there was hope. Now there's nothing.

I set the phone in the charger.

Bile rises in my stomach. I taste the coffee I drank for breakfast.

And just like that my little lifeboat of hope is lost in an even bigger storm at sea.

* * *

Despite my black mood, the weather is gorgeous. No chance of our date with Jon and Molly being called on account of rain. For comfort, I make brownies.

Not necessarily to eat. Cooking soothes me. I think it's because the recipes are a constant in my swiftly changing world. So I cook when I'm happy; I cook when I'm sad; I cook when I'm uptight or anxious or angry. Another form of therapy that doesn't get me in nearly as much trouble as shopping therapy. As long as I don't eat the end result.

I pour melted chocolate into the brownie batter.

It's not a date.

I don't date.

But I'm in the kitchen making another batch of brownies for Jon, and I'm contemplating canceling.

The brownies aren't *really* for Jon. I'm making this batch because I didn't ask him what I could bring to our picnic. I can't greet him empty-handed.

This is so awkward.

I pour the batter into a greased eight-by-eight pan, pop the pan in the oven.

I don't want to assume he's packing a picnic for four—how embarrassing if he doesn't—but I don't want to show up with a supper of my own.

I open the refrigerator and look inside.

I could always make enough for four.

Oh, this is too complicated.

I shut the door.

I should just cancel.

What's wrong with me? Have I become bipolar since separating from my husband?

One moment going to the beach with Jon seems the perfect Sunday evening thing to do, then the next minute I'm on the phone with my estranged husband, hellbent on saving my shattered marriage.

I put the kettle on for a cup of tea. Check the clock—one-thirty.

Corbin didn't call back.

Good. I don't want to talk to him anymore. I was an idiot for calling.

What was I thinking, considering chalking the affair up to being one of the hazards of holy matrimony, investing in some heavy-duty marriage counseling and putting him on a short leash for the sake of keeping our family together?

Momentary lapse of reason.

If I feel myself slipping again, I just need to remind

myself that as Caitlin gets older, she's bound to find out. People are bound to talk.

Didn't your dad have a fling with that Magic dancer?

Okay, maybe that's a little far-fetched, but if she did find out, what kind of a message would it send to my daughter? What would it say about love and respect and the true meaning of marriage? That she's not worth a man's faithful love? That a man with money can get away with anything, including walking all over the woman he promised to love, honor and cherish?

I put my head in my hands and resolve not to cancel with Jon. I will go and have a magnificent time.

Because it will be good for me. That and because when Caitlin was eating her French toast, I made the mistake of telling her we were going to the beach with Molly for a special eclipse picnic. "Do you remember Molly? You two played a few times."

She squinted, looked up at the ceiling, tapped her chin, a gesture she makes when she's really racking her brain.

"Oh, right! I remember her. That was a long time ago. I like Molly. She likes to play Polly Pocket dolls. Will she bring her Polly Pocket dolls to the beach?"

"Probably not to the beach, but maybe one weekend she can come over, and you two can play."

"Can she come over tomorrow since we don't have school?"

"Daddy wants to spend time with you tomorrow. He's taking the day off especially to be with you. We'll ask her daddy if she can come over another day."

"Where's her mommy?"

"Her mommy and daddy live in different houses."

Caitlin frowns. "Oh, did she leave just like Daddy left us?"

The expression on her face breaks my heart, and I want to hold her and say I'm sorry. I'm *so* sorry to do this to you. "We don't have to go to the beach if you don't want to."

She shrugs, a listless manner much too weighty for her six young years. "No, we should go."

As she drags herself out of the room, I can almost imagine her adding, "We don't have anything else better to do."

Mel-o-dy Wentworth's silly little voice laughs in my mind. I hum "I am a Rock" to drown it out.

The phone rings and a big part of me hopes it's Jon calling to say something came up.

"Hello?"

"Kate, it's me."

Corbin.

I tense and strain to listen for his girlfriend.

But I don't hear anything.

"Listen, sorry about earlier." His voice is brusque. "You want me to come over?"

"I did. But your girlfriend helped me realize what a big mistake that would have been."

I slam the phone down in the charger and walk out of the room.

It rings again. I start to ignore it, let the machine get it, but I don't want to hear his voice.

I pick it up, and slam it down again, then push the talk button to take it off the hook so he can't call back.

Since the brownies have forty minutes left to bake, I go upstairs and turn on the water to draw myself a nice hot bath. While the tub is filling, I take off my clothes and scrutinize myself in the full-length mirror.

It's not a nineteen-year-old body.

And then there's those damned small breasts. Would Corbin have stayed if I'd gone to Dave Sander's brother for *the nice set of Ds?*

My waist is still smallish—I'm lucky that way, but my

hips seemed to have spread wider with each child. Did Corbin silently resent that about me? Holding it inside until he just couldn't stand it anymore?

I turn sideways, suck in my gut.

I'll start that ab routine I've been planning to do.

After so many years together bodies tend to mold to one another.

We fit just perfectly together. He used to say that when he held me. *This is my place*.

Does Melody feel new and foreign or has he found *his place* with her, too?

I cross my arms over myself—one over my breasts, the other just below my abdomen. Stare at my slack tummy. I'm a good thirty pounds heavier than when I met Corbin.

Maybe I should diet?

The mere thought makes me hungry, especially with the aroma of the baking brownies filling the house.

How in the world does one ever remember where she misplaced the confidence to take a new lover?

Thinking back, I really don't remember confidence being part of the seduction equation.

It just happens.

Naturally.

So maybe I have a little "interior" design to do on myself before I think about new lovers and relationships.

Because really, the thought is petrifying.

I don't know how, or where to start, or what to do. All I have is what I've known with Corbin and obviously that wasn't good enough. If I keep repeating the same patterns of the past anything in the future will surely fail.

Same sofa.

Different slipcover.

Maybe I'll have these spider veins taken care of—they say the procedure is nearly painless. I run my hand over the red-purple road map on my thigh.

Then again, maybe I won't. Maybe I'll borrow back the hot pink polish I gave Caitlin and paint my toenails.

Yes, that's what I'll do. And I'll even wear sandals to the beach tonight.

I sink down into the warm water and decide that with my small breasts and wide hips and bright pink toes, I will look nice when Jon picks us up.

I'm not doing it for him.

I'm doing it for me.

So much for my makeup boycott.

One of the first things I discover about Jon is he's very easy to be with. He's relaxed and easygoing, a type

B personality through and through. A nice change to
Corbin's tightly wound, type A.

Jon's packed a picnic of fried chicken, potato salad
and coleslaw—which he made himself. In my circles
the men don't cook. I've heard of such an animal that
does, but I really thought it was an urban legend.

He picks us up promptly at four. He brought me a
bouquet of lavender he grew himself in his greenhouse.

"How did you know I love lavender?"

"I just had a feeling."

We pile into his Suburban and listen to Kenny Ches-
ney sing about "The Good Stuff." I've never liked country music. I think it brings me too close to my roots, and
the songs always make me cry. This one was no excep-
tion, and I try my darnedest to hide it from Jon.

He just smiles and sings along. His shorts and Quick-
silver T-shirt, the oversize SUV, his choice of music—
all so different from Corbin. Jon's not into opera or
Corbin's *finer things*.

He seems to find beauty in life's simple pleasures.
One minute it's like balm for my soul, the next it feels
foreign and uncomfortable, and I want to run far away
from it.

Since I'm captive in the front seat of his big truck,

I can't go very far. So I try to relax and remind myself, this is not a date. We are two friends, two parents who are getting their kids together for a play date. Just like I've done hundreds of times with the moms of Caitlin's friends.

Only the moms aren't nearly as attractive as Jon is— well, not in a way that makes me nervous.

I'm glad when we finally get to the beach and have our picnic. It gives me something to do. So I don't feel quite so conspicuous.

It takes a while for me to truly relax, but it happens after dinner when Jon is setting up the telescope and giving the girls a kid-size astronomy lesson.

"Who knows how a star is born?" He winks at me. "No I'm not talking about the old Barbra Streisand movie."

"What?" says Caitlin.

"That was a joke for your mommy."

I smile. This man is perfectly comfortable with himself. Sure, he's good-looking, but I'm sure he's flawed like any human being, even though I have yet to discover those flaws. I'm sure they're in there somewhere.

Still, he's comfortable in his own skin.

You should follow his example, says Hera.

That's all it takes. Well, that and a glass of wine and listening to him interact with the girls while I sit back and relax.

When was the last time I was the one who sat back and relaxed on a family outing? When was the first time?

I realize that I haven't even thought about Corbin since we arrived. Until now.

"Stars begin as a cloud of black dust and gas. The dark masses swirl around out there aimlessly in the heavens until they gather enough particles. But what makes them glow is that they get so many particles going and they're so close together that they get very hot. When the temperature and pressure become too much, they begin to glow. Voilà, you have a star."

The girls are so busy looking through the telescope I wonder if they hear him. But he doesn't seem to mind.

"We're going to see an eclipse tonight. An eclipse of the moon can *only* happen where the moon is full—and you know what else happens on a full moon?"

They look at him. He turns his back, then turns around again quickly with his arms crooked at the elbow and his fingers bent into claws. "That's when the *vare volfe* comes out to get little girls."

Molly and Caitlin scream and run until they fall

down in the sand, laughing and giggling. Jon seizes the opportunity to come back to the blanket and sit down next to me.

I pour him a glass of merlot and hand it to him.

"Thanks." He picks up the container of brownies and helps himself. "Are you having fun?"

I lean back on my forearms and gaze up at the indigo sky dotted with stars that shine like diamonds and at the huge moon that looks like a giant, illuminated penny.

"I am. This is incredible." I gesture to the sky.

"It's as if Mother Nature is slowly pulling a copper-colored shade across the moon." He frowns. "I said that already, didn't I? That's how I enticed you to come with me tonight."

I laugh.

"Darn, I've already spent my best line."

I shake my head. "It is very persuasive. Next eclipse, you'll have to remember to use it at just the right moment. Definitely keep it in your repertoire." I breathe in a deep breath of briny air. "If this were a date, it would be very romantic."

I can't believe I just said that. I don't know him well enough to say things like that. Besides, it's not appropriate to mention dating in front of Molly. She might still be sensitive about her parents' divorce.

But she's not paying the least bit of attention to us. She and Caitlin are back at the telescope, taking turns peering at the moon.

"So it's not a date, huh?" Jon brushes chocolate crumbs from his hands.

I really feel stupid for bringing it up. Stupid and flustered and not quite sure what to say next.

I shrug. "It's still all so new to me."

He picks up the bottle of merlot and refills my glass. "I'm not real good at it, either. Can you tell?"

I sip my wine and watch him over the top of my glass.

"It's just that when I came to change your tire the other day... I don't know, something told me that we might enjoy each other's company. I thought that might be a good place to start. No pressure. Okay?"

As he raises his glass to mine, I wonder what it would be like to kiss him.

All in good time, says Hera.

There's a directness in Jon that's refreshing. I draw a squiggle in the sand with my finger, look up and see him stretching his long, lean legs out in front of him on the blanket.

He leans back and his burly shoulders are as wide as the sky. I've always appreciated a nice pair of broad shoulders.

Girlfriend, if this doesn't prove that you're not dead I don't know what proof you want, says Hera.

The girls come running back to the blanket and fall down alongside of us.

Jon puts an arm around Molly. "See those three stars in a row that are close together? That's Orion's belt. Have you ever heard about the legend of Orion and Merope?"

The girls shake their heads.

"Well, Orion is the hunter. He stands by the river Eridanus and is always accompanied by his faithful dogs because they spend their nights hunting together.

"You see, Orion was in love with Merope. But Merope would have nothing to do with him. One day Orion was so sad because he couldn't get the girl that he wasn't watching where he was going and stepped on a scorpion and he died. The gods felt sorry for him, so they put him and his dogs up in the sky as constellations. They put all of the animals he hunted up there near him—like the rabbit and the bull." Jon points to the heavens. "But they put the scorpion all the way on the opposite side of the sky so Orion would never be hurt by it again."

His story implies more than myth, and I wonder if he's thinking of Pam.

"Is that for real, Daddy?"

"Of course it is. Didn't I just show you old Orion hanging out up there in the sky?"

"But those are just stars, it's not a real person."

"There are all kinds of treasures out there. You just have to know where to look to find them."

He glances back at me.

"The most important thing is if you're ever afraid, you just have to look up in the sky and find Orion and know he's looking out for you."

CHAPTER 13

A week later, my parents come over for dinner. It's the first time they've been over since Corbin left. Between that and Dad's chemotherapy, we're all doing our best to act as if life's normal.

But what is normal?

If there ever was such a thing.

"How's Dad doing with the chemo, Mom?" We're standing together at the kitchen sink peeling jumbo shrimp for scampi. She shrugs and I see a wall go up around her.

"He's doing all right, I guess. The doctor says the first round is always a shock to the system."

I want to ask her to define *all right* because my father looked tired and frail, as if it was all he could do to drag himself in and sit down in front of the television.

"I wish that husband of yours were here right now."

NANCY ROBARDS THOMPSON   219

Mom's lips flatten into a straight line. "I could really use a good unbiased medical opinion."

"Give him a call, Ma. I'm sure he'd be happy to talk to you."

She shakes her head.

I rinse a prawn under the running water and feel a pang of guilt at not having shared the news with Corbin. I'm not sorry for his sake, but for Mom's and Dad's.

After what Corbin's pulled, sharing the news about Dad's condition seems too personal. We don't need his pity. Dad's going to be all right, and we're going to make it through fine, without the help of my louse of a soon-to-be-ex-husband.

I grab another shrimp, pull off the legs and peel back the translucent shell.

"Make a list of questions, and I'll call him for you."

"No, Kate, don't worry about it. You're so busy taking care of Caitlin and preparing for that presentation to the museum. I wish you didn't have to go out and go to work."

"Interior design isn't exactly nine to five. That's the beauty of being my own boss. I can work while Caitlin's in school and after she goes to bed."

My mother does not look convinced. "It's just a shame that with all that money Corbin has—you shouldn't have to work until Caitlin's out of the house. I never worked when you were in school. You never worked when Daniel was at home. I don't think Corbin understands what it takes to make a home. It's a full-time job in itself."

"Mom, he will provide adequately. This isn't about money, don't you see?"

From the look on her face I understand she doesn't see.

"I need to do something that makes me feel like I contribute." How do you explain this to a woman who built her whole life around her family? Who will stay married to the same wonderful man who will cherish her always until death wedges between them and tears them apart? Even then, I imagine, they will part reluctantly. The thought shakes me down to the core.

I'm glad when Caitlin comes in and throws her arms around Mom.

"Look, Grandma, I found this sand dollar at the beach last weekend. It washed up on the shore. Jon and Molly said I could keep it."

"It's beautiful." Mom washes her hands, bends down and puts an arm around Caitlin. "Who are Jon and Molly? Are they new friends?"

"Molly's my friend. Jon's Molly's daddy. He's Mommy's

friend. We went over last night and watched movies with them. Jon said he'd take us to the circus."

She punctuates the words by flinging her arms around my middle.

Mom slants a glance at me, her brows arched. "Oh, I see. Is this Molly a friend from school?"

"Nope. She and her mommy and daddy used to come over for supper, but then they stopped because her mommy and daddy don't live together anymore, just like mine don't."

"Is that right? So you've just gotten back in touch with this Molly?" Mom looks at me when she says it.

Heat creeps up my neck and across my cheeks. I hate myself for it because there's nothing to blush about. "Jon owns an automotive repair shop. The other day I had a flat, and he changed my tire."

"I see. Lucky he happened along."

"He didn't just *happen* along, Ma. I called him."

"Did you call him to arrange the day at the beach, too?"

"It wasn't during the day," says Caitlin. "It was at night."

"You went to the beach overnight?"

This is ridiculous. I shouldn't have to defend myself. I take a can of peanuts out of the cabinet.

"Caitlin, will you take these into Grandpa to eat while he's watching the news?"

"Can I have some, too?"

"Some, but don't eat too many. Dinner's going to be ready in ten minutes. Tell Grandpa that, too, okay?"

As soon as Caitlin's out of the room, my mother says, "Kate, do you really think it's wise to have overnights with men? I mean with your daughter and—well, what kind of example is this setting for Caitlin? You haven't even filed for divorce yet."

I fling a chunk of butter into the skillet, drizzle on some olive oil. It melts under the heat.

"It wasn't an overnight, Ma. We were home before eleven o'clock. Don't you think I have better judgment than that?"

I rake an onion off the cutting board and into the pan. It sizzles.

"It certainly sounds like you're spending a lot of time with him. This is no time to bring another man into the picture to complicate matters. If you have a boyfriend, Corbin might turn it around and use it against you."

I crush garlic with the mortar and pestle, putting my weight into each jab.

"Jon is *not* my boyfriend. I do *not* have a boyfriend."

"Why not, Mommy?"

I whirl around and see Caitlin in the doorway. I don't realize she's returned to the kitchen until I hear her voice. "Daddy has a girlfriend. Her name is Melody."

He promised.

The bastard.

Why am I so shocked that a man who couldn't honor his marriage vows wouldn't keep his word? Maybe I had more faith in him this time because his promise directly affected his daughter.

This morning, I woke up at four-thirty and went over my art museum design presentation until six o'clock. Now I'm standing in the kitchen with the phone in my hand, hesitating like an insecure teenager afraid to call him.

I tried to call him after I put Caitlin to bed, after Mom and Dad left, but he didn't pick up the phone. Most likely *she* was there or he was with her. Must feel wonderful to be able to totally shirk his responsibility. But it's not wonderful, it's disgusting, it's inexcusable for him to act this way.

I left a message asking him to call me as soon as possible, no matter how late it was—that I wanted to talk to him about something that concerned Caitlin.

I guess the naked woman in his bed was much more inviting than an angry soon-to-be-ex-wife.

Daddy has a girlfriend. Her name is Melody.

Anger sears my insides into a hopeless mess. What the hell is wrong with him? Why the hell has he done this to our family? Why do I have to be the responsible one?

I contemplate throwing the phone at the kitchen wall, but instead, I act like the responsible adult I am, take a deep breath and dial his direct line at the office. He should be at his desk, revving up to full throttle right now. That means we have approximately half an hour to hash this out before Caitlin wakes up, and I should still have plenty of time to help her get ready, take her to school and come home to make myself presentable for the meeting at the art museum.

The line rings, and my body tenses. Leave it to Corbin to cause turmoil on a day when I must have a clear head.

I suppose as a single, working mother, I'd better get used to curveballs. They're a part of this new game.

I straighten and steel myself for the ensuing battle.

"Hello."

Finally.

"Good morning, Corbin—"

"This is Doctor Corbin Hennessey, I'm away from

my desk right now, but your call's important to me. Leave a message, and I'll call you back."

I hate that cocky little pause before he starts the rest of his greeting. It's a sadistic joke before he delivers the "psych-out" one-two punch of the rest of the message. *You missed me. Again.*

"Corbin, it's Kate." Barriers of anger harden my heart and voice. "I know you're busy, but this is the second time I've called. I don't understand why you're not calling me back. We *must* talk. It's about Caitlin. I want to hear from you before I pick her up from school this afternoon. I'm taking her to school at eight, then I have a ten o'clock appointment. If you don't get back to me before nine-thirty, call me around noon. But please take five minutes out of your busy schedule to call me. I don't think that's too much to ask."

I hang up the phone.

He knows what he did, and he's hiding because he doesn't want to face me. Then again, right or wrong, when have I ever known Corbin to hide from anything?

A raw and primitive ache overwhelms me because I don't know this man who has no regard for promises. He's certainly not the man I married. No, the man I married was always in the office at the crack of dawn.

* * *

The phone rings as I'm loading Caitlin in the car to take her to school. The caller ID displays Winter Park, Florida and a number I don't recognize, so I answer thinking it might be Corbin calling me back.

But it's not. It's Jon phoning to wish me luck with my presentation today. "Knock 'em dead. They're going to love you."

It's so sweet, Jon's calling me for luck. I can't even get the lousy father of my child to call me back to discuss his daughter. I try to ignore the strange roller-coaster-like dip that makes the pit of my stomach fall out, and not in a good way. This dip is a flag that things are moving too fast, careening out of control.

"Thanks, Jon. I guess I needed that, because I'm a little nervous. I'm kind of out of practice—errr, you know, job interviews."

"Are you kidding? You'll do great."

I wish I believed in me the way he believes in me. More than that, I wish knowing that he believes in me didn't make me squirm. So I file it away with other sweet sentiments he's bestowed on me as if they're tickets I can accumulate and use later for a bigger prize.

"Thanks. I appreciate it, but I have to run or Caitlin's going to be late for school."

"Call me later and tell me how it goes?"

"Sure. Okay."

Call waiting beeps as I'm hanging up. I answer before caller ID has a chance to register.

"Are you all right?" It's Alex.

"Of course I'm all right. I'm running late because the blasted phone keeps ringing, but other than that, I'm just peachy. And you?"

There's a beat of silence, and I feel bad for being so abrupt. She's not calling for the sole purpose of annoying me.

"So… I'm guessing you haven't heard from Corbin this morning?"

The question plucks hard at my tightly strung nerves. How'd she know? I hadn't even had time to vent about Corbin's latest.

"No, and I'm sure right about now he's not too eager to talk to me."

"Have you…heard the news?"

"What news?"

"Oh, great." I detect a trace of panic in her voice. Alex doesn't panic. "Honey, sit down," she says.

I grip the edge of the table. "What's going on, Alex?

My legs turn to noodles as I fear she's about to tell me that Corbin hasn't called me back because he was found dead in his brand-new bachelor pad—heart attack, died on the kitchen counter during rambunctious sex.

"Corbin was arrested last night. It's on the front page of today's *Orlando Sentinel.*"

When will it stop, this revolving insanity masquerading as my life?

Just when I think it's gotten about as bad as it can get, another curveball flies in my face from out of the blue. No surprise I'm striking out. I've never been athletic.

The *Orlando Sentinel* headline, prominently displayed on the front of the local and state section says, "Magic's team physician arrested for DUI."

Oh, Corbin. What's happened to you?

It's enough to make me contemplate curling up in a fetal position until all this insanity is over. But that will have to wait. I'm in the art museum parking lot, ten minutes early for my appointment with the executive director. My lone mission for the next couple of hours is to see the plans for the new museum, pick the director's brain to get a feel for what she and the board have in mind for the new decor, all the while forgetting Corbin is in jail for drunk driving.

Caitlin's with my mother. I kept her home from school today. Since Corbin's antics made the news, some careless parent is bound to blurt—*Isn't that Caitlin Hennessey's daddy?* The child is bound to bring the news to school. Caitlin would be devastated.

I didn't know how to begin explaining the situation to her. I hadn't even properly explained why Corbin and I separated. Just some nonsense about Mommy and Daddy needing a time-out. She still thinks he's coming home someday.

I read a survey that says seventy percent of all married men have at least one affair over the course of their marriage.

I've never cared about being part of the majority.

Sunlight shines through the windshield onto my hands. Old woman hands. When did they become so crepey? My grandmother used to tell me I had pretty hands. When did I lose them?

I make a fist and the skin pulls taut and smooth. Release it and the firm texture gives way to a thousand fine lines that seem even more pronounced now.

How ironic—I can go through life with fists

clenched fighting the inevitable, or I can relax and go with the flow.

Easier said than done.

I make a mental note to buy some hand crème with Retin A, grab my briefcase and make my way to the museum's entrance.

The docent at the desk greets me with a patronizing smile.

"I'm Kate Hennessey. I have a ten o'clock with Marilyn Griggs."

She buzzes Marilyn, sends me into the conference room. I'm a little anxious, but more exhilarated than nervous, really.

About five minutes later a tall, thin, severe looking woman with bleached blond hair cut so short it sticks up all over her head steps inside the room and extends a hand.

Marilyn Griggs eyes me, but does not smile. Chronologically, I'd guess she's in her early thirties, but possesses that corporate barracuda air that makes her seem ageless.

I stand.

We shake hands.

"Where do I know you from?" she says.

I'm fairly certain we've never met, but I review all the lists in my head—Junior League, the Cancer Society, the country club.

"Do you have kids?" I start with the most likely place, Caitlin's school. Kids are always a good common meeting ground.

"No."

Should have known. Not with that figure.

"I was thinking it might be from my daughter's school. Often when I see parents out of context, it's hard to place them."

She stares at me blankly. Okay, no connection there. I should have joined the museum council when Joan McCracken tried to entice me. Corbin encouraged me to.

It will give you and Joan a chance to get to know each other better.

I would have gotten a lot of mileage out of museum council association right now. Although ladies of the council do not work. They dedicate their free time—when they're not lunching or playing tennis or checking in for a plastic surgery or rehab—to philanthropic causes because they need something to fill their time while their husbands golf and fool around. They'd never dream of getting a *real* job.

"Is it possible we've met through Rainey Martin? She's a good friend and a docent here sometimes. She told me about your search for a designer."

Marilyn Griggs shrugs. Sometime-docents, like Rainey, are an entirely different breed from council members. It's on the tip of my tongue to mention Joan McCracken, but her name sticks to the roof of my mouth like peanut butter.

"Did you bring your portfolio?" Marilyn asks.

I hand her my notebook, feeling pretty proud of myself. I sketched a few renderings, laid out several design boards and created a business card and identity for myself—Kate Hennessey Design Studio—after Rainey mentioned the job. I can do this on my own. I don't need to drop names.

It takes Marilyn less than a minute to look through my book. "Anything else?"

I panic. "This is my most recent work. I can provide you with additional designs if you'd like."

She slides it away from her, leans back in her chair and crosses her arms. Her expression floats somewhere between bored and disgusted.

"What have you done?"

Her tone is almost reproachful. It's my turn to stare

at her blankly, uncomprehending. For a moment I'm afraid she's commenting on the mess my life has become and is preparing to lecture me on foolish choices.

"Your work," she snaps. "Tell me about some of the projects you've designed."

My heart pounds—from relief and humiliation for not being more astute.

Well, let's see…for the past seventeen years I've been a stay-at-home mother… I've perfected the art of beige-on-beige, taken it to new heights, actually. You should see what I can do with a bottle of fifty-year-old cognac and a potted plant. Goodbye boring beige sofa.

This does not bode well.

"Lately, my work's been mostly…residential."

She says nothing.

I scramble mentally to fill the silence.

"I just finished the most wonderful Moroccan living room. Spice colors, beautiful tapestry."

She nods, unimpressed. I've never seen a more ex-pressionless face in my entire life. I thought art types were supposed to be colorful and eccentric. Or at least alive. This woman is so boardroom stuffy I expect her to crack into tiny pieces and blow away on the bone-chilling AC draft that's gusting down on me.

Marilyn stands. "Come look at the plans for the new building." I follow her to a table on the other side of the conference room where the blueprints are laid out.

After giving me the virtual tour, she hands me a packet and walks to the door.

"This contains all the specs. Everything you need to know. Call my assistant to schedule an appointment to submit your design to the board next week. We'll make our decision by the first of May."

She wants to see more? Well... Wow. But—

"Do you have any ideas or specifics you'd like to discuss? Any likes or dislikes or general direction for the image you'd like to portray?"

She blinks—twice. "You're the designer. Come up with a plan that will knock my socks off."

Knock her socks off? I'm fairly certain she doesn't wear socks. Or if she does, they're of the painted-on Corporate Barbie thigh-high variety guaranteed never to as much as slip, much less be knocked off.

Oh. I get it. She's being polite asking me to submit a design. Even in her stuffy, unsmiling way, it's corporate courtesy. I took the time to come in. She's not about to slam the door in my face, despite a miserable presentation.

Oh well, the interview was good practice. A warm-up for another job I'm better suited for.

I offer her my card anyway. She snaps her finger and points at me.

"I know why you're familiar. It's not you. It's your name. It's that Hennessey who was in the news today. The Magic's doctor who was arrested. Hennessey. Yes, that's it. Any relation?"

CHAPTER 14

"Jon, I can't believe I lied in a job interview. Isn't that grounds for immediate termination?"

His laugh, soothing and rich, transcends the cell phone static. "Only if they find out. Besides it's not a permanent position. I'm sure there's some civil right that precludes them from judging you by your ex."

I hold on to the phone with my shoulder as I use both hands to make a left turn onto Mills. "I hope so. I wasn't about to tell her the louse was—*is* my husband. It's too complicated. I can't believe this mess Corbin's gotten himself into. It's so embarrassing. He could have killed someone."

"Yeah, just think how *he* must feel."

"He deserves to feel bad."

"Spoken like a scorned lover."

"Hey, whose side are you on?"

"I'm on your side, darlin'. To prove that, I'll buy you lunch. A good burger and cold beer will do you a world of good."

"I can't drink beer in the middle of the day, I'll fall asleep. Plus I have to get Caitlin from my mom's house in an hour or so."

"Call and ask if she can stay a little longer. Or if you want, I'll call her and ask—"

"No. I'll do it. Caitlin was telling her about our trip to the beach and my mother had a conniption."

"Why? Doesn't she like me?"

"She doesn't know you. I'm sure if she knew you she'd love you. What she doesn't like is the idea of me dating before I've filed for divorce. Actually, she's not particularly fond of the whole divorce issue, either. It's a long story."

"Dating, hmm? Is that what we're doing?"

A little rush of adrenaline makes me laugh. "There you go with that word again. I'm going to hang up before you get the wrong idea, and check on Caitlin. I'll call you back in just a minute."

"Darlin', I'll wait right here."

At the next stoplight I dial my mother's number.

"How did it go?" she asks me.

"Dreadful."

"What happened?"

"I had absolutely no chemistry with this woman. In the end she linked my name with Corbin's. It was a disaster."

"Oh honey, I'm sorry. Surely she won't hold you responsible for your ex-spouse's sordid affairs."

Sordid affairs. Yes, that would just about sum up Corbin's life in one broad stroke.

"I'm sorry, dear. I didn't mean—"

"Don't worry about it, Ma."

"Well, listen," she says. "I was thinking—today's Friday and with you under such high stress, why don't you let me keep that little granddaughter of mine tonight? Dad and I would love to take her to the zoo tomorrow. That'll give you some time to unwind, talk to Corbin and figure out how you're going to explain this drunk driving mess to your little girl. Don't you let him push this off on you. He has to take responsibility for his actions."

I haven't been away from Caitlin since this whole ugly business unfolded when I was in South Florida. But I know time to clear my head will do me a world of good.

"Thanks, Ma."

"Well, I'd better run. We have some cookies to bake and a whole fun night ahead of us."

"I'm going to grab a bite of lunch. Then I'll go home and work on this art museum presentation."

"I thought you blew the interview?"

"I did, but she invited me to submit. Probably just a courtesy. Call me on the cell if you need me."

"I don't think businesspeople waste your time or theirs with courtesies. I'm sure we won't need to ring your cell, but it's nice to know it's there just in case. Now go relax. Pick up your little girl around four o'clock tomorrow."

I hang up and call home to see if Corbin's left a message on the machine, but there are no messages. He didn't call me to come bail him out.

Well. It's all for the best.

Half an hour later, I'm sitting with Jon in a little dive pool hall with a banner on the wall that boasts they serve the best burgers in Central Florida. The place is nearly empty except for us and two men and a woman playing pool at a table off in the corner.

I imagine that they're regulars, that the bartenders know them by name. I imagine they think I'm a little overdressed in my pink suit, but I don't care. It feels good to disappear in here, drinking Samuel Adams out of the bottle at noon in this dark, seedy bar that reeks of stale drink and cigarettes and has mock Tiffany light fixtures advertising Miller beer.

It's as if I've stepped into an altered dimension where I don't have to explain or pretend—or lie, while Corbin sits in jail.

I haven't done this since college.

Jon takes a long pull off the brown bottle.

"Why'd you marry him?"

I shrug, tear at the blue-and-red label on my beer. "He swept me off my feet. He's good at that—obviously. No, I don't know, he was ambitious, from a life so different than what I was used to. You know, everything I thought I wanted."

"Was he?"

"Does marriage ever turn out like you expect? As you grow and change you become a different person, want different things. When I married Corbin, it was like I'd been hired for this awesome job that was way too big for me. Most of the time I felt underqualified, and I worked my butt off to transform myself into the perfect doctor's wife. I had babies and kept house and volunteered. Then, twenty years later, I wake up and find myself here."

The Eagles version of "Desperado" comes on the jukebox. I laugh, sip my beer.

"What's funny?" Jon asks.

"This song. It's a little too ironic, don't you think?"

"'Desperado'? I don't think of you as that type. You've always done the right thing and seem to have done a damn good job at it."

"But who am I now? Without this man I've built my entire life around?"

"Only you can answer that. I can tell you what I see."

"No, don't. It was rhetorical, really."

"But that's not as important as who you believe you are. I mean, who do you see when you look at me? Jon Beck, auto mechanic? If so, why are you hanging out with a grease monkey when you're used to men stations above me?"

"I see a man—"

He reaches across the table and presses a finger to my lips. "Shh… it's rhetorical."

He smiles that smile I love so much. "All I know is when I look at you, Kate, I see a woman who deserves more, a woman who is head and shoulders above a nineteen-year old basketball dancer."

"How do you know? You've never met her."

"True. But I know. Believe me, I know."

I reach out and touch his hand.

"You always make me feel so...so wonderful. Thank you."

He turns his hand over so we're palm to palm.

"Darlin', you are *wonderful*. I just wish you could see it, too."

The waitress delivers our burgers and another round of Sam Adams.

Just in time.

As I draw my hand back, my wedding rings glitter, and I retreat into the awareness that Jon and I are teetering on the dangerous edge of a high cliff.

He eyes my rings, and I hope he doesn't ask me why I haven't taken them off.

He doesn't. His eyes travel past them to the ketchup bottle the waitress sets on the table. He fixes his burger and takes a bite.

Maybe it's the beer, but as we eat in silence I feel all aglow, and he's responding with lingering looks and slow smiles.

Part of me wants to grab his hand and take a running leap off that high cliff, but it's too soon since Corbin left, and I'm still as fragile as blown glass.

We sit there talking for a long time, and the place fills up with the evening crowd. The din of conversation gradually increases and the proprietor turns up the volume on the jukebox.

We sit there drinking and talking about everything and nothing. About the travesties of the four hurricanes that devastated Florida last year, about our daughters, tangerine paint and why he's chosen to work on cars rather than put his business degree to work.

"I'm just more comfortable doing what I'm doing rather than dressing up and doing the nine-to-five grind."

I never knew this about him. I mean, I knew he was casual and laid-back, but I never dreamed he was blue-collar by choice.

"It was one of the reasons Pam left me. She thought I wasn't ambitious. She wanted me to be a pharmaceutical rep. But it just wasn't me. I'd be traveling all the time." He winks. "I wouldn't be here with you right now."

I arch a brow. "You might be going home to your wife tonight. Do you miss her?"

He shrugs, signals the waitress for another round. Yikes, how many have we had? With each new round the waitress removes the empties so I've lost count. All I know is I can't feel my nose. I am drunk. But not drunk enough to forget he never answered my question.

"Do you miss Pam?"

"Miss her? Hmm… I miss the way I wished things were. You can't have a child with someone and completely forget. If you can, then there's something wrong." He stares at his hands for a long moment. "Life's a lot simpler now."

It wasn't what I wanted to hear. I don't know, I guess I expected him to be over it, memories filed away in a place that made them inconvenient for perusing. But at least he tells the truth.

I hear the crisp clack of a pool cue hitting billiard balls, the pop of stripes and solids knocking and scattering across green felt, the thud of balls dropping into pockets.

A long-haired man in leather at the table closest to us sinks one. I imagine it's the four ball. I don't know why, but right now I like that number. If I were playing, I would try to hit in number four.

"Do you shoot?" I ask him.

He nods. "Notorious in thirty counties. Do you?"

A mournful country tune wails from the jukebox. I've never heard it, but its sad minor notes strike a melancholy discord in me.

"Not in a long time. Even then I wasn't any good."

He shakes his head. "Darlin', you're so much better than you give yourself credit for. I'm going to show you. Let's play a round." He tips his head, a dare, and gets to his feet, beer in hand.

I grab my purse and he motions to a table in the far corner. I lead the way, feeling his gaze on me as I walk, taking care to cross one foot over the other in what I hope is a sexy stride. I've shed the suit jacket and am very glad I'm wearing the snug skirt and my heels—even if I am a little overdressed for a pool hall.

He racks the balls. "Do you want to break?"

I shake my head. "Go on, I might put someone's eye out."

His mouth twitches a bit on the left side.

He positions the cue ball. "Come here." He steps behind me. I think he's going to wrap his arms around me, but instead, he draws my right arm back and positions his left hand over mine on the edge of the table, and balances the cue over it.

He's so big. His body completely engulfs me. So unlike Corbin's wiry, compact runner's body. Jon is just one hundred percent big, broad man—everything from his shoulders to his chest to his hands. I like the nearness of him, the feel of his hard stomach on my back, the smell of green and Dial soap and laundry detergent. My mind pushes aside Corbin's face to imagine what it would be like to be Jon's lover, but I reel it back to the safe feeling, the security of feeling right and removed from all the world's wear and worry.

I surrender under him and let him pull back my arm, push it forward in a quick shooting motion, until the white ball scatters the pyramid.

He doesn't move. Neither do I. We stand there together, him over me. "There. That wasn't so bad was it?" His voice is low and raspy in my ear.

"No it wasn't. And that's what scares me."

I turn my head ever so slightly to the right. My cheek brushes his. He turns to meet me, his lips brushing mine. It's a whisper of a kiss that makes my heart pound and my brain say *oh no*, but his lips taste like beer and something indefinable—something male, and despite the alarm going off in my head—that I'm kissing a man who is not my husband, in public—I don't want him to stop.

It's a leisurely, slow kiss that starts with lips and hints of tongue. Until he pulls me out from under him and turns me so that he can deepen the kiss. I slide my arms around his neck and open my mouth, fisting my hands into his hair to pull our bodies closer.

On one level, I kiss him because I enjoy the feeling of being alive again, having a man touch me and respond to me, and on another, deeper plane, I am seeking refuge in his arms, healing all the hurt we've both suffered at the hands of careless lovers.

"Let's get out of here," he says, his lips against my ear, on my neck.

He pays the check and we step into the cool night air.

I'm relieved when he recognizes that we've had too much to drink to drive and calls a cab.

We stand in a strange sort of aroused limbo as we wait for the car outside the bar. The humid night air and the traffic whizzing by reminds me that we are no longer sheltered by the dark pool hall world that poses no threat.

Out here, cold reality rushes by in shiny cars. I glance at my Lexus sitting in the parking lot and imagine it sitting there abandoned in the morning. I feel an uneasy pang.

I think Jon knows this, because he smiles from his post, a respectful distance away.

"I'll bring you back in the morning."

What are we doing?

When the cab arrives and we are tucked safely inside, he takes my hand, lifts it to his lips. All the guilt and worry that ballooned a few moments ago floats up and out of the car and we ride to my house in a fever of anticipation.

CHAPTER 15

Twenty minutes later, the taxi stops in front of my house.

"You're coming in?" I ask.

He gives me a knowing smile, shakes his head. "There's nothing I'd like more, but I'd better say good-night. Come on, I'll walk you to the door."

It's odd, this feeling that swirls through me. I'm both disappointed and relieved, which only proves I'm in no shape to ask him in. Because I know where that path would lead, and I fear where we'd find ourselves in the morning.

He asks the driver to wait. Walks me to the door.

My hand is shaking as I insert the key into the lock. My mouth is dry as we step into the hall and close the door. Jack barks and jumps. He needs to go out after being in all day, but I'll see to him in a moment.

Right now, all I can do is appreciate Jon's discretion.

He just seems to anticipate and understand without my having to explain. I long to tell him to let the cab go, to stay with me tonight.

"When it happens, it's going to happen right," he says, as if reading my mind. "Not like this, after we've spent the day drinking beer, which was fun, mind you." He takes my hands in his, pulls them to his lips. "I don't want to do anything that's going to make life more complicated for you."

My stomach sinks because I hear the part he's not saying, *You're married and vulnerable, Kate. I don't want to complicate my life.*

"This sounds like goodbye."

A soft smile spreads over his mouth.

"Are you kidding? We've barely said hello. I'll bring bagels in the morning, we'll go get your car. So get a good night's sleep so we can get an early start."

He kisses me, slow and smooth, then pulls away and opens the door.

As I wave goodbye to this man who takes time to notice the moon, and grow lavender in his greenhouse, I'm both grateful and sorry that he has enough willpower and good sense to do what's right.

I push the door shut, and walk upstairs alone, sliding my wedding rings from my finger.

When I get upstairs, I put them away for the last time.

In the morning, I lay in bed for thirty minutes trying to decide if I'm hung over or just mortified that I spent the entire afternoon in a pool hall drinking beer and sucking face with Jon while my mother watched my daughter and my husband sat in jail.

I sound like a candidate for the *Jerry Springer Show*— is he still on television allowing people to publicly humiliate themselves? If not, I'm doing a good job without him.

I lay my arm over my eyes to block out the fresh morning light hoping I can go back to sleep, but the phone rings. I roll over to answer it and glance at the clock— Seven o'clock.

"Hello?"

"Good morning," offers an incredibly sexy voice.

I remember why I was tempted.

I'm flooded with relief that Jon did not wake up sober and regret yesterday.

"Hope I'm not calling too early," he says. "I heard a notorious pool shark plied you with beer all afternoon yesterday."

"Good news travels. I was all set to let him take advantage of me, but he'd have no part of it."

Jon laughs. "What's wrong with that guy?"

"I hear he has a conscience."

"The death of many a good rogue. Are you up for getting your car?"

"Jon, you don't have to come all the way over here—" I prop myself up on my elbow. "Out of curiosity, how would we get there? You left your car there, too."

"Nothing like a good run to get the blood pumping early on a Saturday morning."

I fall back and put my arm over my eyes. "Oh, no. I'm definitely not up for a run."

"Good, I'll drive you. I ran over and got my car."

"It's seven in the morning and you've already worked out. I knew I'd eventually find something wrong with you."

"It was only five miles. Worked out all the poison I put in my system."

"Lucky you. Do you do that often?"

"Run or poison myself?"

"Both?"

"I run just about every day, don't make a habit of overimbibing, if that's what you're worried about. Only when a beautiful woman knocks me for a loop, and I'm trying to think of a way to prolong my time with her. I honestly can't remember the last time that happened. I'm rambling, so how about if I bring over these bagels I just picked up, we'll have a quick bite, and I'll take you to your car?"

"Jon. Whoa. Are you always this talkative in the morning?"

"That would be a problem, right?"

"Uh-huh."

"Then I'll hang up now. See you in thirty."

I barely have enough time to shower, dress and put on coffee—no makeup; hair will just have to dry naturally. Coffee outranks beauty this morning. Besides, Jon saw me in all my natural glory the day he changed my flat and came back for more. I'm not worried.

Well…maybe just a touch of mascara.

I'm on my way upstairs, when the doorbell rings. Jack goes crazy barking.

I'm caught off guard by the way my stomach flutters. When I glance out the peek hole and see Jon standing there, I'm sure the way my stomach feels has nothing to do with the afteraffects of the beer.

"Good morning," he says. His right arm is braced

against the door frame. He carries a brown bag in his left. My newspaper is tucked under his left arm. His hair is still damp and curling around the collar of his white T-shirt. I imagine this is what he looks like after he's just gotten out of the shower—only with clothes on.

"Come in. Please. Good morning." Now I'm rambling. Stammering, actually.

Jack jumps up and licks Jon.

I grab the dog by the collar and see Betsy Farmer across the street in her driveway. She's staring. Blatantly. No doubt, she's heard about Corbin's troubles, knows we've separated. I'm sure all the neighbors know by now, but no one's called. I'm glad. Really, I am.

Pariah is the word that comes to mind. *Can you believe what happened to Corbin Hennessey?*

What a bunch of hypocrites.

I'm not defending Corbin or justifying what he did. But they all do it, go out to dinners and parties, have cocktails, a couple bottles of wine, a little cognac. Then they get in their cars and drive home because they can *handle it*.

I'm sure they're all breathing a sigh of relief—*better Hennessey than me*. Some of them might even be careful for a couple of weeks—stop after a couple, name a designated driver—but all too soon they'll revert to their old ways.

Betsy waves. I'm sure she's trying to figure out how Jon factors into the equation. Corbin moves out, gets arrested; tall good-looking guy in green Suburban shows up on Kate's doorstep. I wonder what Betsy would do if I kissed him?

I glance at Jon's lips, wave at Betsy and close the door.

"Mmm, that coffee smells good," says Jon as he follows me into the kitchen. Jack tries to break away and jump on Jon.

"Come on, Jack, want to go outside?"

I shove the dog out the back door. Jon stands in the middle of the kitchen, holding the brown bag of bagels at his side, glancing around the blue-and-yellow room.

I go to the sink and wash my hands.

"After I finish redecorating the bedroom and master bath, I'm going to tackle this room."

"What would you do? It looks great."

I set two plates and silverware on the table, and look at my kitchen trying to see it through his eyes. I shrug. "I haven't thought that far ahead. I just want something different. It's good to mix things up every once in a while. I haven't redecorated in years."

He nods, seems a little stiff. An awkward air passes between us, as though neither of us knows quite what to do next. I wonder if all his telephone bravado was to cover up how unsure he feels.

I know I'm feeling a little strange.

We crossed *that line*. Where do we go from here?

"Sit down." I pull out a chair—the one I usually sit in, not Corbin's—put the sugar bowl on the table, walk to the refrigerator to get the half-and-half.

He holds on to the back of the chair, but doesn't sit. "Kate, I don't know how to say this—"

I glance at him over the open door, and I'm not sure if the chill passing over me is from the icebox or those eight fateful words he uttered.

I wait, half-and-half in one hand, the other on the top of the door.

His throat works in a swallow. "I'm just going to say it." He rakes his hand through his hair. "I had a great time with you yesterday, but I don't want to blow things by rushing into something you're not ready for."

I let out a breath and do a quick litmus test: is this his way of backing toward the door or is he giving me an out?

I shut the refrigerator, pour the half-and-half in a creamer and set it on the table next to the sugar.

He's standing not three feet from me, and I'm suddenly aware of his height and hulking breadth. I have to tilt my head to look him in the eye.

"I don't know what I'm doing right now, Jon, and it's going to take a while to sort it all out. I just know that I like spending time with you."

I don't know who moves first, but we're in each other's arms. The worry that woke me early this morning slides away as I kiss him and he kisses me back. His lips are on mine. His hands are on my face, in my hair, on my body, pulling me into him. This time as I drink from his lips I taste pure want and dangerous, thrilling lust.

It cracks open the hard outer shell that's formed around me over all these years. The genuine me, the me I used to be, steps out and drinks in the first real taste of life she's had in years. As I slide my hands down the hard planes of his back, I remember how it feels to be impulsive and wanton, totally and completely selfish.

Taking something just for me.

I may not know what I'm doing, but I do know I want this man. I want him naked and in my bed upstairs.

Or maybe I'll take him on the kitchen table—have him for breakfast rather than the bagels.

Or maybe…

His kisses wash over me like the smell of brownies baking, like the sound of the rain falling outside my window. Being in his arms is like lying on the cool grass and staring up at a starry sky, feeling a million miles away from everything, as if nothing in the universe can harm me.

Maybe I'll just stay right here for a while—

In the recesses of my mind I hear a door shut, feet shuffling on wood, the growl of a voice—

"What the fuck's going on in here?"

We jerk apart.

Corbin's glaring at us from the doorway.

CHAPTER 16

Corbin's a smart man. I'll give him that much. But you'd never know it when he swings his balled fist at Jon, who outweighs him by a good fifty pounds.

Jon blocks the punch as if he's swatting a gnat and says, "You don't want to add assault and battery to your rap sheet." Corbin turns and punches the wall, then lets fly a string of words that makes his frequent use of the F word sound like poetry.

Jon steps between Corbin and me. Jack is barking and throwing himself against the door as though he'd take someone's head off if he could get in.

I shake my head, "Let me handle this." I contemplate asking him to leave so Corbin and I can hash this out.

"That's right, Beck. Get the hell out of here. Keep your fucking hands off my wife."

"Excuse me?" I step to the side so I can see Corbin. "Jon's staying, and I am not your wife anymore."

"I haven't seen any divorce papers." Corbin's hand is already starting to swell and turn purple.

"You initiated divorce when you slept with Melody."

"So is that what this is about?" Corbin points to Jon. "Tit for tat? I screw a cheerleader, you fuck a mechanic?"

Jon lunges toward Corbin.

"No!" I wedge myself in between them. "Jon, you go in the living room. Corbin, you leave. You have no right walking into this house without knocking. You can talk to me through my attorney."

"It's *my* fucking house. I'm not leaving, and I'll walk in any time I damn well please."

"It's not your house. You gave it up when you left your family for a woman the age of your son. Now get out before I call the police."

I pick up the phone.

"How did you get here, Hennessey?" Jon says. "Did you drive?"

Corbin's eyes flash, and for a minute I think he's going to swing at Jon again.

"Corbin, I'm serious. If you're not out of here in ten

seconds, I'm calling the police—if the neighbors haven't heard us and called them already."

I press the talk button on the phone. Corbin hesitates; the ramifications seem to settle around him.

Corbin mutters something unintelligible, grabs the edge of the table and upends it, then storms out, leaving the front door open.

I hear the squeal of tires peeling out, Jack barking and my heart pounding as I stand amidst the broken dishes and scattered bagels.

Why do I feel like the one who was caught cheating?

I've done nothing wrong.

You're damned right you haven't, says Hera.

Oh, shut up. You're the one who tried to convince me to give Corbin a second chance.

Okay, so maybe I was wrong. Even a goddess makes mistakes. You could cut me some slack and focus that aggression where it belongs.

I know she's right.

It's time I put an end to this.

After Corbin's chest-banging territorial outburst, Jon offers to change the locks for me. I say I'll call a locksmith to rekey, but he won't hear of it.

"That'll cost a fortune," he says. "Why waste the money when I can do it for you?"

He has a point. We leave it that I'll cook dinner tomorrow night. The girls will have a chance to play while Jon changes the locks. Maybe I'll have him show me how. I should do one. It can't be that hard.

Saturday, after Jon takes me to my car and leaves, I go to Home Depot before I pick up Caitlin from Mom and Dad's house. I will buy four new dead bolts—one for each of the doors, so they'll all be keyed the same— and a new garage door opener.

It's another world inside that hardware supermarket, with its wide aisles and aroma of fresh-cut lumber.

Let's see. Locks…that would be aisle number six. Thanks to my redecorating projects I'm learning my way around the hardware store as well as I know the mall. Which reminds me, I need to look at tile for my new studio. I've decided to rip out the carpet and tile the floor in what used to be the guest room. That way I can work with paint and glue if I want to do mosaics, and I won't have to worry about getting it on the carpet.

I've turned the room that used to be Corbin's old office into a guest room-playroom for Caitlin. She loves it.

While I'm here, I believe I'll ask the manager what they do with their chipped and cracked tile. Take something broken and turn it into something beautiful.

I steer my cart to the tile section and pull from my purse a drawing of Hera I created. I love the vivid cobalt, bright turquoise and true, clear reds, yellows and greens.

This is it. This is my mosaic.

I load a case each of tan and cobalt tile into the cart. It's not cheap. I'll have to buy the tile a couple of cases at a time until I have all the colors I need, but this should get me started.

Yes, this will do nicely.

I make my way over to aisle six and look at the daunting display of shiny brass locks. But with a little help from my orange-aproned friends, I get what I need and am on my way to get my daughter.

There's something very unsettling about needing to lock out a man to whom I've given twenty years of my life. But there's something very fulfilling about picking out and purchasing my own hardware.

When I get to my parents' house, Dad's still in bed. He's been there all day.

"Is he okay?"

"We didn't make it to the zoo. He's just too weak, and I was not about to go off and leave him."

"Mom, why didn't you call this morning? I would have been here earlier."

Mom shrugs, brushes a piece of gray hair off her forehead. She looks weary.

"I hate to tell you this," she says. "The doctor has asked Hospice to come tomorrow."

Fear balloons inside me. "Do you need me to stay with you tonight?"

"No, baby. You take that little girl home and spend some time with her. She is such a joy. But before you go, why don't you go in and say hello to your father? I'll get Caitlin's things together."

I knock before entering the dim room, but he doesn't stir. Pausing in the doorway, I can barely make out his form on the Shifman bed, but I hear his labored breathing.

It sounds like death.

I feel my insides fold in on themselves.

Daddy, please be strong. What is Mom going to do without you? What will we all do without you, because you're one of the last honorable men left in this world?

* * *

Two weeks later, I'm putting the finishing touches on my museum design boards when Alex calls.

"Do you want the good news first or the bad news?" she says.

I push down on the tile sample I'm gluing to the art museum presentation board. "There's bad news? God, Alex, I don't think I have any room left in my life for bad news."

She sighs, and I feel my calm start to crumble like dry clay.

"Well, it's not devastating news," she says. "It's just that—shit, Kate, I screwed up. I can't believe I've let you down like this."

"What? What's wrong? You're scaring me."

"I called Sarah Martin over at Long, Drake, and Martin. She's the best in the business. If I were getting divorced, she'd represent me. I told her I was referring you since I can't represent you, and told her to go for Corbin's balls because you're my best friend."

She pauses, and I wonder if I'm missing something.

"Okay..."

"Kate, Corbin's playing dirty pool. There's an ethics policy that says if one party in a divorce consults with an attorney, even if they don't hire said attorney, that lawyer is disqualified from even talking to the other party in the case. Corbin consulted with Sarah."

"So? Who would be your second choice? That's fine, I'm not really out for blood here. I'm mad at him, but I don't want to crucify him."

"Well, you might want to after you hear this. There's an old trick in this business—to keep the spouse from securing a good attorney, the other will consult with every decent lawyer so the spouse who's not so fast out of the gate is left with the bottom of the barrel. It's dirty pool, but that's what Corbin's done. I'm kicking myself for not seeing it coming."

"Why would he do this?"

"He doesn't want you to have a fair shake. He wants you to get some hack who'll be an easy mark for his ballbusters. In short, he's hoping that you'll end up paying him."

"That's ridiculous."

I stand up, walk to the door and look out at the backyard. It's a lot brighter out there since the Carters killed the tree. The stark midday light glares down on the grass like a flood lamp. Is there no human decency left in this world?

"Alex, I'm not good at this. I don't want to fight, but I certainly don't want to get taken advantage of. Come on, all I want is a decent life for my daughter. I am the mother of his children. For God's sake, I'm getting a job."

"Honey, after twenty years you deserve a lot more than that. When this happens, most people will settle for someone they can get locally, but Corbin underestimates us. That really pisses me off. I'm going to set you up with Dennis Lauder out of Miami. He's a good guy. He'll do right by you."

The presentation of my design to the museum board goes marginally better than my one-on-one with Marilyn Griggs.

There's safety in numbers.

When one board member refuses to make eye contact because she is picking at her cuticles the entire time or the most senior member flat-out falls asleep, I can scan the room for an interested face.

Finding sanctuary, however, is harder than I hoped, especially when the sleeper interrupts my explanation of why I recommend tile over carpet by snorting himself away.

I keep telling myself the exercise is good practice.

It's an honor to be included in the final round of presenters.

Right.

Who am I kidding?

This is not the Oscars.

CHAPTER 17

Hera may be the goddess of all goddesses, but I have something she doesn't: the treasure of Alex and Rainey.

It's Caitlin's night for dinner with Corbin, and the girls have come over for a renovate-the-guest room-into-a-studio party. I've made spinach dip and sangria. We have Ottmar Liebert on the stereo, a gallon of azure paint for the walls, and this crazy game Alex brought over for after we finish our work.

"Jon sounds like a dream," says Rainey.

We each painted one wall. Now she's helping me lay out mosaic tiles in the design of Hera I drew on the reverse side of some gummed paper, while Alex finishes the last wall. The goal of putting the mosaics on paper is that when we finish, we will lift the completed design to glue we spread on the wall, peel off the paper and voilà—instant Hera mural.

"A guy who cooks, changes locks, and is down-to-earth enough to care for a six-year-old sounds like a god," says Rainey.

"Yeah, but let's cut to the chase," says Alex. "Is he good in bed?"

I run my hand over the pile of black tile pieces, select a skinny rectangular section and stick it down on the area that will be Hera's hair. "I haven't slept with him."

Rainey drops a tile. "And why not?"

"It's not because of Corbin, is it? I always say what's good for the goose," says Alex.

I sigh. Shake my head.

"Good," says Rainey. "When can we meet Jon?"

A sickening wave of claustrophobia passes over me and threatens to strangle me with its sticky fingers.

"I don't know if I'm ready for all this, you guys. Maybe I should wait until the divorce is final."

Divorce.

Even after all these months, the word still leaves an aftertaste like cayenne pepper. It makes me want to choke.

Alex frowns. "How will that help matters? Your marriage has been over for a while now."

I sigh. "It's just…"

Hera's face—half mosaic, half paper—smiles up at me

from the design template. I wish I were more goddess-like at this stage of my life, but right now, I just want to put a pillow over my head or numb myself with sangria.

Hera says, *Great, you've become a forty-year-old, divorced alcoholic. Girlfriend, this is not good.*

I push to my feet, pour myself another glass of wine and turn to face my friends. "I'm not sure where things are going with him. I don't know if I want to tie myself down to someone so soon after leaving one relationship. I guess I'm having trouble because this isn't where I wanted to be in life when I turned forty."

Rainey gets up, walks to the bowl of chips. "Is anybody where they thought they'd be?" She licks spinach dip from her fingers. "I mean, look at me. All Hank does is watch television and doze on the couch when he's not working. Ben's going off to college in the fall, and I have no idea what I'm going to do with myself."

"I'm happy," says Alex.

Rainey and I glare at her.

"Well, you suck," says Rainey.

Alex shrugs. "Life's what you make of it. I'm turning forty, and I haven't spoken to my mother in ten years. And I've never been married. Some people would label my life a total mess. But I choose to see the good.

Life's a hell of a lot more peaceful without Zona pulling her antics, and I have a thriving law practice that keeps me way too busy to get involved with anyone long-term. It's all in how you view it."

We silently contemplate the idea for a minute.

"Oh gag," says Rainey. "When did Pollyanna step in and what did you do with our old cynical Alex? We want her back."

"Hey, watch who you're calling old." Alex stands in the middle of the blue room, hands on hips. "I'm serious. People are calling forty the new thirty. I like that, because if we're looking in askance at how we got to this juncture in our lives, ten years ago we were totally clueless. Personally, I'd feel pretty cheated if the best years of my life had gone by and I'd missed them because I was so worried about arriving at the wrong station when I got here."

Rainey frowns. "I guess. And if we can't age gracefully there's always BOTOX."

We laugh.

"Let's take a break and play this crazy game I brought." Alex pulls a small book with a psychedelic cover out of her purse and holds it up. It's called *Zobmondo: The Outrageous Book of Bizarre Choices*.

"Let's get away from these paint fumes and go out into the living room," I suggest.

We grab the chips, dip and drinks, file downstairs and settle on the pillows in the living room.

"Here's what you do. The game pairs two weird situations. You're supposed to choose between the two and tell why." She stares at the cover. "I didn't realize it before, but I think this game is particularly appropriate in light of the bizarre and outrageous fact that we're each turning forty this year."

She lifts her glass. "To the fearless forties."

We clink. "Hear! Hear!"

Alex opens the book at random and fires a question at Rainey.

"Would you rather lick a frog or a public toilet?"

I almost drop my sangria.

"Disgusting!" says Rainey. "Neither, thank you."

I cluck my tongue. "No, you *have* to choose one. Don't be a party pooper."

"I want another question."

"No," I say. "Let's make a rule that you have to open the book at random and that's your question. No picking and choosing."

Rainey rolls her eyes, then weighs the pros and cons of frogs and public commodes.

Alex scoops some spinach dip onto a tortilla chip and drums one hand of perfectly manicured acrylics on the coffee table. We look at Rainey as if she's about to reveal something earth-shattering.

"I have no idea how you can eat spinach dip with those horrific choices on the table," says Rainey. "Contemplating myself performing either of these two acts has made me doubt whether I will ever be able to eat again. Not that it would be a bad thing." She pats her belly.

"You're not fat," I say. "Don't be ridiculous."

"You're a pal, but I am definitely carrying around way more meat than is considered chic these days. Sometimes I can kid myself into believing my curves are lush and voluptuous. Given how into my body Hank is these days, most of the time, I simply feel fat."

She closes her eyes and scrunches her nose. "Ughhhhh. Frog or toilet? Okay, I'll take the frog. Because sometimes I have a hard time even using public toilets for what's intended, much less getting more intimate."

Still grimacing, Alex nods in support of her choice and slides the book across the table at me. "Your turn."

I take the book and start to flip to a page when the phone rings. I consider letting the machine pick up the call, but wonder if it might be Caitlin calling.

"Excuse me for a sec." I lay down the book and walk into the kitchen.

"Hello?"

"Kate, it's Mom." Her voice breaks on the last note.

"What's wrong?"

She starts to say something, but it's broken by an anguished sob. My blood goes cold. And I know.

"Is it Dad?"

"Honey…he's dead."

When I see Jon standing on the porch with a bouquet of flowers and a white teddy bear, all I can think about is Mom's upstairs resting—she's taken a sedative the doctor prescribed—and I don't want her to wake up and find him here.

It's crazy, I know. But she doesn't approve of my dating before I get the divorce, and I don't want to be the cause of any more stress in her life right now.

"Kate, I'm sorry."

His words make me cry. He hugs me, but I feel nothing. It scares me not to feel anything. It's as if I'm made of ice and have frozen so solid it's killed all my nerve endings.

I pull away when I hear feet on the stairs. I'm relieved when it's Caitlin coming down to see who's at the door, not Mom. Jon hands me the bouquet, and I bury my face in the blossoms not wanting my daughter to see my tears.

I didn't make her go to school today because she was awake several times last night crying over her grandpa. Between what's happened with Corbin and this, she's missed more school in the last month and a half than she missed all year last year.

"Did Molly come with you?" she asks, hopeful.

"No, kid, she's in school. It's just me and this bear today."

He drops down to one knee and pulls her into a hug, then gives her the bear.

"I'm sorry about your grandpa. I'm sure he loved you very much."

I have to do *something* or I'll lose it. So I walk into the kitchen and pull out the big Waterford vase.

A wedding present.

I feel as though I should give it back. One less thing to divvy up.

I hear Jon and Caitlin chatting in the foyer. I can't make out what they're saying over the water I'm drawing for the flowers, and the crinkle of the paper as I remove the wrapper.

Just as well. I don't want to hear him consoling my daughter. Because that might warm me and melt the ice that's numbed me against all feeling.

The flowers are not the lavender from his greenhouse that I like so much, but a professionally grown bouquet of white lilies and roses.

It's while I'm trimming the stems at perfect forty-five-degree angles that I feel Jon's hands on my shoulders.

"What can I do, Kate?"

I shrug.

I don't know what to do. How can I tell him what to do? Nothing anyone can say or do will make a difference.

He turns me around, puts his arms around me. When he tries to kiss me, it's as if I'm a third person in the room watching myself pull away.

I turn back to the flowers, shove them all down into the vase—cut or uncut—and put them on the table. "Thank you for the flowers. They're lovely."

Jon stares at me. I can tell by the look on his face that he's bewildered by my pulling away from him.

"I'm sorry. I— It's not you. I just need—I just need a little time. There are so many things in my life that are broken right now, Jon. I don't know how to deal with anything anymore."

"Kate, let me help."

I shake my head. "Nobody can help. I just need time to help my mother through this, time to help Caitlin get used to all the changes."

He nods, but his eyes are sad. "I've said from the start that you don't get over a twenty-year marriage overnight. Take all the time you need. But Kate, please, don't get so wrapped up in helping everyone else that you forget to take care of yourself. Okay?"

With bittersweet regret, I watch Jon walk out the door.

Hera says, *Girlfriend, you are making a huge mistake. That's one of the finest men you're ever going to meet. I just hope you realize it before it's too late.*

CHAPTER 18

Dad's funeral unfolds like a three-act play.

Act one: We arrive at the church, and Mom falls apart.

Act two: Corbin shows up. He and Daniel, who flew in from Berkeley last night, take charge, greeting guests, accepting condolences on behalf of the family, acting like the men of the house.

Act three: As I help Mom from the mourning room into the sanctuary, I spy Jon over the sea of faces, sitting in the last pew. He gives me a rueful smile and nods. I haven't talked to him since he brought the flowers three days ago. The way Corbin is acting, I know it must appear that we're back together. Still, I can do little else but let him carry on, because Mom needs me.

None of the relatives, who have flown in from all over the country, know that Corbin and I are separated. In a perverse way, I'm almost relieved for the illusion that everything is status quo in our house so that it does not divert attention from the funeral. This is a day about remembering my father. Not a day for whispers like, *You know the Conrad family never had a divorce until Bill and Mary's only girl. I'll bet he's rolling over in his casket.*

So I let Corbin be the man; and I let Jon sit in the back; and I let my mother cling to me because she needs me.

The rest of the funeral is a blur of flowers, hymns, Bible passages and recollections of my father.

He was cremated, so there's no burial—we will gather in the fall to scatter his ashes at sea, just as he requested.

At the end of the service we follow the minister down the aisle. As we approach Jon, Corbin has the audacity to put an arm around me as if he cares. I sidestep away from him as if I'm moving into position to better secure my mother's grip on my arm.

Corbin shifts to the other side of her and offers his arm. My mother, bless her heart, angles away from him, and I sense a silent stab of contempt.

He quickens his step to get the door for the procession.

Oh, so helpful and attentive.

He makes me sick.

When we form our receiving line in the lobby, Corbin goes to settle with the minister. Jon is one of the first to come through.

"I'm sorry, Kate, Mrs. Conrad."

As I watch him walk out the church's glass front doors, I'm sure that if I could feel anything, I'd regret letting him walk away. I might even go after him.

Go after him, urges Hera.

"Who was that?" Mom's watching me.

"That's Jon Beck. He's the father of Caitlin's friend Molly."

Her gaze searches my face. "Oh, I see."

I glance in the direction of Jon's exit, but he's gone.

Rainey and Alex skip the funeral to keep Caitlin and make sure everything is ready for the after-service reception.

I hope Jon will come, but am not a bit surprised when the last guest leaves and he hasn't shown. It would have been awkward with the way Corbin is making himself at home.

I try to be understanding since Daniel is home for such a short time, and I know he wants to see his father. Corbin and Daniel sit on pillows in the living room—my Moroccan living room, thank you very much—talking for a long time.

Then later, Corbin comes into the kitchen and starts helping me clean up what the caterer did not.

"How are you doing, kiddo?" he says.

Kiddo? Since when does he call me *kiddo?*

I have an urge to ask him if that's his pet name for Melody—Hmm, where is Melody today, and how does she feel about Corbin having so much *family time?* But I don't ask because I really don't care.

He stands beside me at the sink and picks up the dish towel that's lying on the counter. "Daniel's upstairs making some phone calls. I'll dry."

As we stand side by side doing dishes together, I can't remember a single time in our twenty-year marriage when we did something as simple as this.

I realize with startling clarity that this man is a stranger.

"Where's your mom?" he asks.

"Upstairs resting."

He wipes a wineglass, sets it on the counter. He acts as if he's going to take another, but he grabs my hand instead of the glass. I pull away and in my haste, the glass slips from my grasp and shatters in the sink.

"Oh!"

"Don't worry about it." His hand is on my arm, now. I shrug it off. I don't have the energy to get into it with him right now.

"Kate, please. If I've learned one thing since your dad died, it's how short life is. Your father's death has reminded me that life is fragile and fleeting. Unlike that wineglass, it can't be replaced."

I squint at him because I have no idea what he's getting at. All I know is if he says one more word about *death* I'm going to scream.

"It feels good to be home again—in my house, in *our* house." He takes me by the arms and turns me toward him. I'm so aghast at his referring to it as *my house, our house*, that it takes a few seconds to register when he says, "Kate, I'm still in love with you. I want to come home."

I open my mouth to protest, but he's already talking.

"I screwed up. I miss my family, and I want us all to live together again. I will go to counseling, anything to work through this."

"Corbin, this is hardly the time to be talking about this. I—I can't even think right now." I take two steps back. So there's enough distance between us for me to breathe. From this distance I look at the man who is the father of my children, the man who promised to keep himself only unto me until death do us part, and I try to imagine what marriage would be like on this side of the affair.

Lots of marriages survive infidelity. Lots of women pick up the shattered pieces and put them back together stronger than they were before. I guess I'm just not of that ilk.

"So, I take it that Melody's out of the picture?"

He sighs, twists the dish towel, nods.

"Who left who?"

"That's not important. What matters is that we're—"

"Who left who, Corbin?"

"She left me, but I was going to break it off with her if she hadn't moved out. I'm being honest with you."

"*Moved out?* You were living together?"

"She's not *half* the woman you are, Kate."

The girlfriend's gone? He wants to come back? Just like that? As if I should welcome him with open arms, like the dutiful wife?

"Frankly, Corbin, I can't believe your audacity. You had your little fling, now you want to come back? I don't think so. You blew it, and this time, I'm not going to be the one who fixes it."

"What? Is it Beck? Do you two really have something going?"

How typical. That he would think me incapable of standing on my own two feet.

"I think you should leave."

To my surprise, he slinks out of the kitchen as if I've beaten him. But I'm the one who feels bruised by life's whiplash ride of late: Corbin's cheating; these feelings for Jon; Dad's death; Mom's moving in; losing Jon.

For a second I have a panic attack—will life ever be right again? Or will it just keep spinning out of control and will I just keep falling from one plateau to the next?

I hear Corbin at the front door.

"Corbin, wait a minute!"

He's standing in the foyer, looking hopeful, when I get there.

"How did you get here today?"

He looks puzzled, but smiles. "I drove."

He drove. Despite the arrest, despite the suspended license, he drove. Now he's getting ready to walk out and get in his car despite the drinks he's had at this afternoon's reception and drive himself away.

"I thought the only reason you were supposed to drive was to get yourself to and from work?"

He snorts. "If I get pulled over, I'll just tell them I have an emergency at the hospital. They'll never know the difference."

Oh my God. His words reach all the way down to the pit of my stomach.

"That line fools them every time, doesn't it?"

"Oh…Kate. I—" He reaches for me.

I shake my head.

"Goodbye, Corbin."

CHAPTER 19

It's only been a month, but in some ways it seems as though my father's been gone forever. The memory of him settles around us like a fortress. His presence is larger than life and always with us.

That's why I'm caught completely off guard the day my mother informs me she's taken an apartment in a retirement community.

We're sitting at the kitchen table having a sandwich, talking about what we'd like for dinner—we've fallen into a nice, comfortable routine of working together in the kitchen—when she drops the bomb. It goes something like: "We could have rosemary pork chops or chicken picatta for dinner tonight. By the way I've taken an apartment, and I'm moving out at the end of next week." I nearly choke on my ham and cheese.

"There is no reason for you to live alone, Mom."

She gazes at me over the top of her glasses. "I appreciate your letting me stay with you, sweetheart. But it's been a month now, and I think it's time I got out from under your feet."

"You are *not* under my feet, and if I have done anything to make you feel that way, I'm sorry."

"Your divorce is final. It's time you got out, started dating, started living your life. You're not going to do that if I'm living with you."

I finger the handle of my mug and consider this.

"And to tell you the truth," she says, "I don't think your Dad would want me to tuck myself away on a shelf, either. I'm going to travel. One of the things that made me decide to take the apartment at West Oaks Village is that they have an active travel club. Next month we're off to Ipanema, Brazil."

She holds her arms like a flamenco dancer and snaps her fingers like castanets.

I want to be happy for her —that she's gathered so much strength to forge ahead. But I can't just yet. I'm stuck back at the starting block having just come to terms with her moving in with me, of me taking care of her, of her *needing* me.

"Katie, don't look at me like that. You've lived in

emotional purgatory far too long, and it's time you moved on." She takes my hand. "Just because one relationship ends doesn't mean life is over. Just as the end of your marriage doesn't mean *you're* a failure in life. The only thing that brands one a failure is letting opportunities for happiness slip by unrealized.

"I loved your father and will grieve for him for a long time—maybe for the rest of my life—but I want to travel and live the next chapters of *my* life as fully as I can."

As my mother sips her tea, I have a moment of clarity. It's not so much that I'll miss her *needing* me. I'll miss the friendship we've forged. We've always been close, but in this month that we've lived together, we've surpassed the mother-daughter relation and become friends. We've shared the precious jewels of ourselves we found as we've sifted through life's rubble. We've polished them, strung them together and worn them proudly like a beautiful necklace on the way to forging this intimate friendship.

That is what I will miss most about my mother not living with me. But I know she is right. I know it is time we moved on.

I start to tell her so, but the phone rings.

"May I speak to Kate Hennessey, please?"

"This is she."

"Hello Kate, this is Marilyn Griggs from the museum. I'm calling with good news. The board loved your presentation and would like for you to design the interior of the new building."

Several weeks later, I'm lying down with Caitlin waiting for her to fall asleep. I stare at the dark ceiling and remember the time Jon told the girls how a star begins as a cloud of black dust and gas. *It has to build a lot of pressure before it can shine.*

Ha! How very ironic that is.

When Caitlin's breathing reaches the rhythmic pattern of slumber, I get up, walk to her window and look out. It's a clear night and stars twinkle in the sky, but her window faces west so I can't see what I'm looking for.

I go downstairs. Jack follows me outside. Dragging a chair into the yard, I search the southern sky. For a minute I can't find it, but then I see it—the three stars close together: Orion's belt.

I fall into the chair and sit there for a long time staring up at it.

Tomorrow, I'll be forty.

With all that's happened over the past months, I've certainly earned *star status*.

I have a new career; Mom's become the girl from Ipanema—at least she's standing on her own two feet. Obviously, I didn't give her enough credit.

My divorce is final. Corbin showed great decency by not contesting the agreement. It was a clean, simple break, which was a little bittersweet considering the twenty years of our lives we gave to each other and the way he was all set to move back in after Dad's funeral. But it's best this way. Those years are not gone. I will tuck away the memories, like photos in an album, and pull them out occasionally. There may be years that I don't bother to take the album down from the shelf. But they'll always be there when I choose to remember.

It's such a clear night. I can see the stars that form Orion's head.

I swear one of them is winking at me.

Jack is exploring the far corner of the yard. I leave him outside as I go in and get the phone.

I settle back in my chair, take one last look up before I dial Jon's number.

My heart beats like the wings of a caged bird. I

haven't talked to him since the few brief words we exchanged at Dad's funeral.

He may not want to talk to me.

I'm a little disappointed when his answering machine picks up.

After the beep I say, "Hi Jon, it's Kate. I was sitting here looking at the stars, and I was thinking about Orion and his woman, Merope. She made a big mistake giving up a great guy like that. But you know how stars are—they have to go through a lot before they can really come into their own. Merope knows that now. She had a great guy and...well, she blew it. But I couldn't help but hope if Orion really cared for Merope, maybe he'd give her a second chance?"

After I hang up the phone I go upstairs to bed. I walk down the hall to my studio to turn off the light. Hera smiles at me from her place on the wall.

You don't need me anymore, sister goddess, you're just fine.

And for the first time ever, I really believe it.

I'm forty today.

Mom and Caitlin spoiled me the entire day. They scheduled a day of beauty at the Euro Day Spa. I had a massage, an aromatherapy hydro treatment, which boiled down to a big whirlpool tub spiked with delicious essential oils. The bath was in a candlelit room, Enya played on the sound system, and I sipped cucumber-lemon reverse-osmosis water—whatever that is.

After that I had a manicure and pedicure.

I feel like a new woman—or maybe this is how forty is supposed to feel?

It's off to a good start. I talked to Rainey and Alex first thing—a three-way conference call over which they sang "Happy Birthday." I loved it, but I told them not to quit their day jobs—I know, it's pretty unoriginal to say that, but they have many other good qualities that make up for their lack of musical talent.

Hey, I guess you can't have it all. But we sure can try.

Jon didn't return my call, but I'm not surprised. I mean, what did I expect? I'm not going to dwell on it, but despite everything that happened between us I hoped I might hear from him today.

I guess I get a little sentimental when it comes to birthdays. But not everyone feels the same.

If I've learned one thing this year, it's that no matter how well you think you know someone, you never really know them. The only person you can rely on is yourself.

I hope that doesn't sound bitter, because I'm not.

Really.

I've reached a calm. Maybe it's all the to-do that surrounds turning forty. Once you're there it's anticlimactic. But that's all right.

So now that I'm bathed, massaged, manicured and thoroughly relaxed, Mom—who is tanned and lovely, freshly returned from the Ipanema beaches—Caitlin and I are on our way to dinner. My favorite restaurant, Bella. Always a treat, but tonight with my two special girls, the experience will be superb.

Mom valet parks the car.

We step inside. I love the beautiful Italian marble floors and the frescoed walls. Mmm…and the smell of the wood-burning oven. I hang back while Mom speaks to the maître d'. I'm sure she's taking the opportunity to advise him it's my birthday. I'll be a good sport. At least here they don't embarrass the celebrant too badly by making a spectacle of her.

The maître d' smiles at me. "Happy birthday. Right this way."

Can I call 'em or what?

"What are you in the mood for?" Mom asks as we walk.

I smile. "I've had my heart set on the salmon. I've been looking forward to it all day."

We enter the back room.

"SURPRISE!"

What—?

"Oh my God—"

I see Rainey and Alex and a sea of balloons and—

"Daniel?"

He hugs me. "Happy birthday, Mom."

I hold him at arm's length and look at him because I can't believe he's here. "When did you get in?"

"I flew in about an hour and a half ago. Rainey picked me up from the airport."

"We've only been here about twenty minutes. For a while, I was afraid we wouldn't make it before you did," Rainey says.

Alex hugs me. "I was afraid I was going to have to call your mom and have her come up with a good excuse to waylay you."

"How about a glass of champagne?" The voice comes from behind. Its deep, rich timbre reminds me of a spring night at the beach, under a blanket of stars. It courses through me like the tide lapping over the shore.

"Jon."

I turn. He offers me a flute of bubbly and a smile.

"Happy birthday, Kate. You look beautiful. You're glowing."

"I thought—"

"I'd have called you sooner, but I was afraid I'd spoil the surprise."

I take the champagne, and he kisses me on the cheek.

The seven of us sit down to a lovely dinner and dessert. After the last present is opened and the last good-bye is said, Jon offers me a ride home.

"You go with that handsome man," my mother says. "Take her out dancing or somewhere fun. I'll take the kids to my house—all three of them. Molly, would you like to spend the night, if it's all right with your daddy?"

She nods and looks at Jon with hopeful, pleading kid eyes.

"It's fine with me."

I look at Daniel, not wanting to leave him so soon after he arrived. "But—"

My son holds up a hand.

"Go, Mom. I'm going with Grandma. I'll see you tomorrow."

After we leave the restaurant, Jon drives to Lake Osceola near Rollin's College.

We park, and he takes my hand as we walk down to

the dock. A full moon shines on the water, and the faint scent of jasmine hangs in the air, heady and sweet.

"I got you something for your birthday."

"Jon, you didn't have to do that. Your being here tonight is enough."

He pulls a parchment scroll tied with a pink ribbon from his jacket pocket. "I had a star named for you."

His words steal my breath. I open the scroll and see the certificate from the International Star Registry.

"Oh, Jon. How beautiful."

As we walk to the bench at the end of the dock, he says, "I had a heart-to-heart with Orion. I'm pretty sure I've straightened him out about Merope—if she'll still have him."

I smile. "I have it on good authority that Merope may want to take it slow, but she welcomes this Orion character into her life with open arms."

He kisses me long and slow.

When we take a breath, I look up and see a star twinkling in the southern sky, or maybe it's just a glint in Jon's eyes. Whichever it is, I am certain it's a sign that life *does* begin at forty.

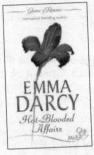

0507/23b

MILLS & BOON
Special Edition

On sale 18th May 2007

THE MATCHMAKERS' DADDY
by Judy Duarte

Zack Henderson was starting over. But he hadn't
planned on falling for Diana Lynch. He knew she and
her two adorable matchmakers were better off without
a man like him…

UNDER THE WESTERN SKY
by Laurie Paige

When compassionate midwife Julianne Martin was
accused of stealing Native American artefacts, investigator
Tony Aquilon was sure he had the wrong woman…

DETECTIVE DADDY
by Jane Toombs

Fay Merriweather was in labour when a storm stranded
her on the doorstep of detective Dan Sorensen's cabin.
He gave Fay and her baby the care they needed, but he
never intended to fall for this instant family…

MILLS & BOON®

Classic novels by bestselling authors for you to enjoy!

PASSIONATE PARTNERS

Featuring

The Heart Beneath
by Lindsay McKenna

&

Ride the Thunder
by Lindsay McKenna